"You're in danger," Gage managed to say.

"You're delusional from the lack of oxygen," Rachelle said.

She had *no* idea, he realized.

In the next moment, the doctor affixed an oxygen mask over his mouth. Relief swept over his pained body, but not his mind. He needed to make sure Rachelle was safe before he was completely incapacitated and unable to protect her. The female pirate could come through the front door right now and take them all out, and he wouldn't be able to do anything to stop her.

He whipped the oxygen mask off his face. "You're in *terrible* danger."

"I didn't rescue you so you could kill yourself." She replaced the mask on his face and kept her hand there so he couldn't move it. Her glittery green eyes locked on his.

He tried to tell her to stay with him. The idea of him begging anyone, never mind a woman, to stay beside him, felt foreign but somehow comforting.

Regardless that it was for her safety, he liked her there.

It made him feel as though he had family.

Books by Katy Lee

Love Inspired Suspense

Warning Signs
Grave Danger
Sunken Treasure

KATY LEE

is an inspirational romantic suspense author writing higher-purpose stories in high-speed worlds. She dedicates her life to sharing tales of love, from the greatest love story ever told to those sweet romantic stories of falling in love. She is the children's ministry director for her church as well as a leader of a Christian women's organization. Katy and her husband are both born New Englanders, but have been known to travel at the drop of a hat. As her homeschooled kids say, they consider themselves "world-schooled." But no matter where Katy is you can always find her at www.katyleebooks.com. She would love to connect with you.

SUNKEN TREASURE

KATY LEE

HARLEQUIN® LOVE INSPIRED® SUSPENSE

Recycling programs
for this product may
not exist in your area.

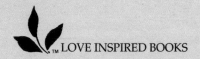 ™ LOVE INSPIRED BOOKS

ISBN-13: 978-0-373-44621-6

SUNKEN TREASURE

www.Harlequin.com

Printed in U.S.A.

He reached down from heaven and rescued me;
he drew me out of deep waters.
He rescued me from my powerful enemies,
from those who hated me and were too strong for me.
They attacked me at a moment when I was in distress,
but the Lord supported me.
He led me to a place of safety;
he rescued me because he delights in me.
—*Psalms* 18:16–19

To Jason, my blue-eyed gentleman.
You bring me so much joy with your quick smiles
and caring heart. I love you beyond measure.

Acknowledgments

First, I want to thank my editor, Emily Rodmell.
Without her brilliance, I would be laughed at.

Second, a huge thank-you goes to the Scuba Shack
and to Enfield Scuba for their training and expertise
that gave me the knowledge to write the dive scenes
with accuracy and feeling. Any mistakes are my own.

And third, as it is on Stepping Stones Island,
community is just as important in my life. I want
to thank my church community at Calvary Church.
Your support means the world to me, and not only
with my writing, but in every aspect of my life.
God bless you all abundantly.

ONE

"Oh, no you don't," Rachelle Thibodaux said with her camera held steady at her eye. From her boat and through her telephoto lens, a diver could be seen holding a Thibodeaux lobster trap in his hand, swiped right off the ocean floor. The poacher, dressed in a black, full-bodied wet suit, jumped up on the diver's platform of a luxurious mega yacht with his dinner in hand. *Her* dinner. "Get your own bug catchers," Rachelle grumbled. "Judging by your ride, you can afford it." She let her camera fall back to her chest where it found its perpetual home, hanging on the strap around her neck. "You're going down for stealing my pots." Well, not technically her pots, she begrudged, but her uncle's. She sped up her turtle-slow, thirty-two-foot lobster boat that also belonged to him. She had a poacher to catch before the thief made off with her livelihood.

Stolen lobsters only increased market prices, and in turn, that meant sales lost to the competition. Which also meant lost jobs. There was no way she could lose this job because of another's crimes. The idea of more undeserved penalties being slapped on her shoulders brought on an unusual wave of seasickness, even with the sea around her at a dead calm. She supposed a year of paying for the sins of her father was what brought the nausea on so quickly, but it was the idea of having to take a job on the island again that really unsettled her stomach.

Because it would also unsettle her life…again.

Images of this past year's disapproving faces aimed at her had her pushing the throttle to its fullest speed, a race to catch a thief before he ruined everything. Her job at sea allowed her to live on the Island of Stepping Stones after her father's tsunami of an arrest knocked her facedown.

Literally.

She didn't think she'd raised her head and looked an islander in the face since the sheriff carted her father away—and the islanders had turned their shocked and accusing eyes on her.

More waves of nausea doused her, but it was the wave of panic that had her reaching to the locked drawer on her right and pushing the four-digit code to release the latch. She had to make sure her job at sea remained intact… whatever the cost.

Fidgety fingers opened the drawer where a black revolver with a rosewood handle lay alone, looking sinister and lethal. Her uncle Jerome kept it aboard for protection purposes. Traversing the ocean alone left one vulnerable. Hijacking, shark attacks and—case in point—thievery could occur at any moment. But even so, Rachelle winced at the idea of picking up the gun. She wouldn't shoot at anyone, she reasoned. If she used it, it would only be to shoot it in the air to stop the poacher in action. It would show the thief she meant business.

Her hand curled around the revolver's handle and stilled. Could she really shoot a gun at all? *Should she?* What if it awoke a part of her better left undisturbed? The part that proved it didn't matter how well she behaved or how isolated she made her life out here at sea. That deep down, the islanders were right. She was just like her father.

A killer.

She relinquished the cold, wooden grip and, instead, snatched up her camera again. The only thing she would be shooting today was pictures.

Rachelle brought the boat to a standstill and raised the black SLR. The diver filled her viewing screen, and Rachelle brought the thief up close and into focus. "Turn around so I can see your thieving face," she said under her breath while she set the camera to shoot off multiple shots in a row for that split moment when the diver turned toward her.

Click. Click. Click.

The diver froze.

There was no way the mechanics of the camera could be heard from this distance, but the rumbling of her lobster boat's motor could be. With one leg still in the sea and the other on the dive platform, the diver lifted his face and turned.

"Smile for the camera, you—"

Rachelle cranked her focusing ring to bring the diver's face into full frame, unsure if what she viewed through the lens was real. *Could it really be?* Was her poacher a *woman?*

Long, curled lashes swept over a pair of flashing, gray curved eyes. *Definitely a woman.* Not even the diver's mask could hide the feminine glare through the lens. For a brief second, Rachelle's finger stilled over the shutter release, then remembered this chick was a thief. It didn't matter if she was a female. Gender played no role in the ability to sin. A lesson Rachelle gave herself daily.

She took the shots at rapid speed before the thief threw the contraband into the boat and disappeared inside. Through the viewfinder, Rachelle zipped around the yacht looking for her or perhaps another person somewhere around the deck and sails. Did the thief work alone? Rachelle took a few shots of a black flag with some sort of words scrawled across it at the top of the mast. She also snapped a few of the boat's name painted on the stern. The *Getaway*.

How appropriate.

A spike in temperature boiled Rachelle's blood. This poacher would *not* be "getting away" with her crimes any longer.

Rachelle dropped her camera back to her chest and accelerated her boat's speed again. The engine kicked in, rumbling as the bow plowed through and sliced the dark ripples of rolling waves.

She expected the thief to take off, but the yacht remained anchored. The distance between them shortened. Rachelle wondered if the poacher had a conscience and was in the middle rethinking her devious deeds, but then a popping noise wrenched through the air and all thoughts flew from Rachelle's head as millions of tiny pieces of sharp shards from her pilothouse windows flew in at her.

Sent careening backward to the floor, she sat there dazed, her eyes scrunched, her arms raised to shield her face. After opening her eyes, she realized she'd let go of the wheel in her fall—and the boat still moved. She got to her knees in a rush to grab hold of the throttle and halt the boat from moving forward. Her hands shook on the handle…and bled.

Bright crimson gripped her attention. Blood. Her hands dripped with blood. *Her* blood. *What happened?* Her mind was muddled with confusion. Then another window blew inward. More glass shards spewed over her like a blanket of sharp needles. Her mind awoke from its tangle in an instant. Only one thing could be powerful enough to obliterate tempered glass.

A gun. The thief was shooting at her with a gun. And these were not warning shots. They were meant to kill… or at least stop her from chasing anyone down. Rachelle's forehead stung where the shards penetrated her skin as if they were the bullets coming at her.

Rachelle eyed the radio above on the dashboard. Did she dare get up to make the call? But she couldn't sit here waiting for—

The hull jolted with another hit.

Would it ever end? Rachelle whimpered at the realization that it would only end when the shooter found her mark.

Crouched low, Rachelle covered her head with her hands. A sprinkling of glass fell from her hair to her thighs. The sharp edges, glinting with her blood, transfixed her. This was really happening. She had to do something before it was too late. It had to end before she was killed.

She got to her knees. Her thick rubber coveralls protected her legs from the blanket of glass beneath her. After today, she would never again complain about how the oversize trousers looked like orange whale blubber on her.

If there *was* an after today, anyway.

Without lifting her head above the dash to give the shooter a target, she fumbled for the radio above. Pain punctured her palm where she touched more glass covering the top of the unit. Rachelle gripped her lower lip in her teeth. Her shaking fingertips found the receiver, and as she twisted around and leaned her back against the console, the receiver's spiral cord pulled tight across her face. Her position kept her hidden from flying bullets and gave a clear view out to the aft deck where today's catch filled large, blue buckets. She'd gladly give the bugs up to the poacher in exchange for her life. The woman could have them all.

With two hands she brought the radio microphone to her mouth. "Mayday! Mayday! Mayday! This is Rachelle Thibodaux on the Rita Ann. I think I'm 54 degrees— No, I'm not sure. Um…I'm drifting two miles due east off Stepping Stones Island. Someone's shoot—"

One black-gloved hand and black diver's hood appeared at the starboard side of her boat. The shooter was coming aboard!

Rachelle let go of the receiver to grab the gun drawer. The radio's spiraling cord yanked the mic back in fast action to some unknown place above, but all Rachelle could focus on was getting the gun. This time she had no choice but to brandish the weapon.

And use it.

Her fingers tripped over the key code.

Access denied.

She didn't dare look away from the neoprene-covered head partly exposed on the other side of boat's wall.

But the diver had yet to move an inch. The woman still hung off the side.

Rachelle took the extra moment to try the code again. The latch clicked successfully this time. On an exhale of breath, she pulled the drawer wide and found the butt. Her hand slipped comfortably onto the grip. Something she would question later when this was all over. And there *would* be a later.

She brought the gun to her chest and realized her camera still hung there. Careful not to hurt her burning scalp more, she pulled the strap over her head and dropped the piece of equipment beside her. Her first time ever not securing it in a safe place.

On her knees, she pointed the gun at the top of the intruder's head peeking above the side wall. "I've got—" she squeaked.

"Help me…" A deep, male voice cut her off. "Please. Someone. Help. I'm injured."

A man's voice. Not a woman's.

This wasn't the woman diver. So the woman *did* have an accomplice. And now he was here to finish the job. "Go away!" Rachelle yelled.

"Please…" The man's distressed voice caused Rachelle to lower the gun a few inches. Maybe he *was* hurt. Maybe he wasn't with the woman, after all.

Yeah, right. Because two divers just happened to be diving in the same exact location with only one boat in the water. They were two miles from shore. Both divers had to have come out on the *Getaway*.

"I've got a gun, and I will shoot you if you board," she warned loudly, glad to hear the only squeaking now was the seagulls above.

"I can't hold…on. Help." The gloved hand slipped from the railing and disappeared. A small splash of water proved the ocean had taken him back in. All signs of the intruder vanished.

Rachelle squinted and leaned forward. She was wrong. Not *all* signs were gone, she could see.

She studied a bright red coloring smeared on the railing. The same color that dripped from her hands. It stood out in stark contrast against the pale yellow of the boat. If the man really was injured, then Rachelle knew exactly what he left behind.

Blood.

I can't leave him out there if he's hurt, she reasoned under her breath. First, he would drown for sure, but second, if he was bleeding, the scent would invite a whole other killer—the blue sharks seen recently hunting these warm, summer waters.

Without dropping the gun, Rachelle crawled to the

starboard sidewall and backed up against it, staying low. Slowly, she pushed up to peer over the railing out of the corner of her eyes.

Gone.

She squeezed her eyes and swiped away the hanging black strands of her hair that had fallen from her ponytail. A huge wad of guilt socked her chest, and she slumped back to the floor. "I let him drown. I killed him. I'm capable of murder after all. I'm no better than my father."

She looked at the gun and dropped it from her hand as though it burned her. Her breathing picked back up, and tears filled her eyes. She squeezed them hard again and let out a wail of fear and tension.

And gut-wrenching disappointment.

"Help!" The voice was back. Distant and at the stern of the boat now.

Rachelle stilled her breathing and listened for the man. He wasn't dead. She could still save him. She scrambled aft, keeping her head low to avoid being target practice for the poacher on the *Getaway*. It hit her that the shooting had stopped. Had the woman left?

Rachelle raised her head a little to search an empty sea in all directions. The setting sun glinted off the glassy water and rippled in peace, oblivious to the nightmare happening around her.

Relief washed over her. The woman was gone.

"Hang on!" Rachelle yelled out. "I'm coming."

She tried to stand, but her legs gave out. She crawled on her knees the rest of the way to the stern. Pulling up on the railing, she saw the man floating on his back, his mask in place but any diving equipment gone. He must have dropped his tank so it wouldn't weigh him down.

"Sir! Reach your hand to me." She leaned over the side,

praying he would hear her. *God, please let me help him. It's not for me. It's for him.*

He rolled to his side in the water, not following her orders.

"Give me your hand!" she yelled again.

He jerked, and his eyes flashed wide behind the mask. His arms flailed a bit before he made contact with her palm and latched on. His powerful grip nearly dragged her overboard, but she'd hauled enough pots up from the seabed to know how to brace herself for the weight on the other end. At least he wasn't dead weight, yet. One big heave and she had the man halfway up the wall. Another pull and he flopped down on the deck, her biggest catch ever.

She whipped his mask off his face. "Where are you injured?" She asked the question while her frantic fingers searched for tears in his wetsuit. She expected to see the neoprene in shreds judging by the extent of the man's incapacitation. All she found was a rip in his forearm. "Is your arm the only place you're injured?"

"Bent," he whispered, his eyes closed and face strained.

"You're bent?" She heard her voice rise and tried unsuccessfully to lower it. The man had decompression sickness? He'd resurfaced too fast, causing a sudden drop in pressure that led to nitrogen bubbles forming in the blood and tissues of his body. It caused severe pain and disorientation. "Why would you do that to yourself?" she screeched. "First time diving? I've never dived in my life, but even *I* know you're not supposed to rush to the surface!"

His head lolled back and forth. "No choice. She cut the hose to my tank. Then cut me."

"She? The poacher?"

"Not poacher." His head fell to his side, his pale lips thinned and tightened. Dazed, cloudy blue eyes found hers, then sealed up tight again. With scrunched eyes, laugh lines around his eyes popped out, not from mirth, though, but from pain. With gritted teeth, he forced out, "She's not a poacher. She's a pirate. And she just stole my boat."

When Gage had woken up on his yacht that morning, little did he know today was payday. He supposed fifteen years was a good run. He had just hoped for a little more time on earth, or rather at sea, since that's where he lived his life on the run.

The girl shouted something in his face, reminding him that he wasn't dead yet. It was only a matter of time, though. If the bends didn't kill him today, there was always someone else who would try their hand at the deed tomorrow.

"Answer me!" the girl yelled again.

Gage pried his eyes open through the pain squeezing his legs. He didn't have an answer because he didn't know her question. All he knew was that one of Marcus's underlings had succeeded in tracking him down. He must have slipped up at some port along the way. Let his next destination slip out. For two years now, he'd known they'd been closing in, but never did he expect to find one of them at the bottom of the sea waiting for him.

The girl kneeled over him, her eyes as piercing and beautiful as cut emeralds. He felt his lips curve into a smile. *"Joyas radiantes,"* he mumbled as his delusional mind evoked fond recollections of one of his favorite sunken treasures to set free from the sea floor. Radiant jewels. Emeralds to be exact. He loved to rescue them from deep waters, as he himself had once been rescued by God.

And now he would be going home to spend eternity with his merciful rescuer.

The girl jostled him to reengage back into this life. He

moaned in response, when he really wanted to tell her to let him go.

"Who is that woman?" It was the voice of the girl, not God he could hear. "What is she doing on Stepping Stones? She shot at me and tried to kill me."

Kill her? Gage pulled back from the peaceful place he felt hovering so near. A peaceful place that couldn't be an option for him today. Not if he brought even an ounce of harm to this innocent young woman.

Gage pried his eyes to slits, pushing past the pain squeezing his skull. He attempted to sit up but realized a wool blanket stopped him. The girl must have put it on him. Nice, but not important. He forced his eyes wide and noticed the blood on her face and hands. Not his blood, but her own.

No, God. Not an innocent person who has nothing to do with this. This has to end. Please make it end.

Gage yanked his hands out from under the blanket to reach for her. "Where are you hurt? Your head is bleeding."

The girl pushed his hands away. "Don't worry about me. It's just cuts from the glass. I'm fine. Just tell me who she is and why she's here. And who are you?"

He started with the question that hurt the least. "I'm… Gage Fontaine. I hunt down shipwrecks."

"And the woman?"

"Jolene. She's also a hunter, but a different kind."

"What does she hunt? Sharks?"

"She would say yes to that."

"What would you say?"

"I'd say we'd better get out of here…before she comes back."

The girl's lips pinched. "Fine. I'll let you evade my questions for now. You're injured, and I need to get you to the clinic. But I'll want to know the truth later, and so will the sheriff." She vaulted to her feet. "So don't go dying on me yet."

"I'll try not to, but the bends can be deadly."

Her emerald eyes flashed in worry, and with a nod she raced to the wheel. The boat began to move swiftly through the water, and all Gage could do was lie there and think. Why would Jolene shoot at the fishing woman? Bringing in the authorities was the last thing these people wanted. It didn't make sense. Unless Jolene thought the fishing woman could identify her. That would be the only reason to kill her. But if that was the case, then Jolene wouldn't rest until she succeeded.

Gage aimed the direction of his eyes to the fishing woman's back as she efficiently brought the boat into shore. Her dark hair was matted to her head in knots and blood, proof of the near-fatal trials on her boat today.

All because he'd brought his dangerous life on the run to her shores.

Gage's stomach rolled with a nausea that had nothing to do with the bends. Fifteen years of running was enough to make anyone sick.

And now he had to tell the innocent fishing woman that *her* days of running had just begun.

TWO

Gage's legs burned along with the aching pain resonating in his knee joints. He needed oxygen fast, the alternate treatment to being recompressed. It was doubtful that this isolated island, surrounded by a barricade of huge rocks, had a hyperbaric recompression chamber in its clinic. It would be forty-eight hours before he would know the extent of his decompression sickness. Shorter if it was worse than he thought.

Gage remembered the day the *Getaway*'s previous captain died. Pete Masters didn't make it thirty minutes after resurfacing. He never regained consciousness after Gage pulled him out of the water.

But death wasn't an option for Gage today. Not with the lobster woman being in danger because of him. He couldn't leave her behind to deal with the pirates. She'd never survive.

Gage flailed his head from side to side. He wouldn't cause another death. He still carried Pete's death on his back like the empty oxygen tank he'd unknowingly geared Pete up with before he took his last dive.

The burden propelled Gage to assess his body as the gurney carried him through the front glass doors of the clinic. He felt pain in the joints of his legs. None in his arms or shoulders. He moved them a bit to prove it. Minimal pain throbbed in his head, but no burning in his chest. Thank the Lord, he didn't have the chokes. His lungs filled to the max with his deep breaths and released with ease. He breathed fine.

"Stop moving. We're here."

Gage opened his eyes to find the fishing woman beside him. Had she been there the whole time? "What's your name?" he asked through his clenched teeth.

"Rachelle Thibodaux." She grabbed his hand where he gripped the edge of the stretcher. Calluses rubbed over his skin, but not unpleasantly. Her evidence of hard work soothed him more than any smooth-cut diamond. He took in the dried blood on her face and more worry for her safety had him trying to sit up. "I said don't move!" she said, and pushed at him.

"Listen to me," he forced out. "It's important. You're in danger."

"You're delusional. Lie down."

In the next moment, the doctor pushed him down and he and his staff transferred him to a bed, affixing an oxygen mask over his mouth. Relief swept through his pained body, but not his mind. He needed to make sure Rachelle was safe before he was completely incapacitated and unable to protect her. Jolene could come through the front door right now and take them all out, and he wouldn't be able to do anything to stop her.

He whipped the oxygen mask off his face. "Rachelle, don't leave here."

"Are you crazy? Put that back on. I didn't cart you all the way here just so you could kill yourself." She replaced the mask on his face and kept her hand there so he couldn't move it. Her green, glittery eyes locked on his. He tried to tell her to stay with him. The idea of him begging anyone, never mind a woman, to stay beside him, felt foreign but somehow comforting. Regardless that it was for her safety, he liked her there. It made him feel like he had family.

The thought stumped him. Maybe she was right, and he *was* delusional. Maybe he had a worse case of the bends than he thought, after all.

As the oxygen broke down the nitrogen bubbles in his affected tissue, he could almost feel the blood beginning to flow freely again. Pain ebbed, and he allowed his eyes to drift closed, if only for a moment. Just for a moment, he said to himself, then reopened them on a gasp.

Everyone who had stood beside him was gone. Vanished in a mere blink of an eye. He searched the room with one sweep.

A different room than before.

His gaze fell on an IV stuck in his arm. His knife wound there was bandaged as well. Not remembering when any of that had happened, he realized he must have been out for a while. Not just a moment like he had allowed.

Even when so much could happen in just a moment.

"Rachelle!" Gage shot up in bed and reached for the IV to rip it out.

"Hold it right there, Mr. Fontaine." An officer in a green uniform stepped into the room. "I want a word with you."

"Rachelle!" Gage's voice reached out into the waiting room with an urgency she didn't understand. Why did this stranger want her by his bedside? She was nothing to him. Nothing to anyone.

Her hands were gripped tightly in her lap as she eyed the glass exit doors, contemplating an escape route. She'd navigate a direct path for her boat and… No, that wouldn't work. Her uncle was already working on getting the windows repaired. He said he should just install bulletproof glass this time. As though this was some kind of a track record with her family.

But then, maybe it was.

Eighteen years ago, Uncle Jerome had lost his wife to a brutal murder. The killer went free and unpunished until last year when the sole witness to the crime brought justice to the island—and changed Rachelle's life forever.

No longer could she work as head hostess at the family's establishment, the Blue Lobster restaurant, the place she thought she would own someday. Baseball caps and sunglasses became her everyday attire so she could avoid the uncomfortable and even condemning stares when she passed people in the street. Her life of solitude, working out at sea, allowed her to survive and provide for herself and for her mother without the constant reminder that it was her father who had caused this change in her life. It was her father's choice to take his sister-in-law's life that changed her own so drastically.

"Rachelle! Are you here?" The diver's frantic voice yanked her back to the present circumstances and the fact that someone else had nearly taken another life today. Two if she counted her own, but right now, the only thing she counted were the seconds ticking away while this Jolene woman escaped punishment for her crimes. The idea of another criminal getting away caused her blood to bubble up like the diver with the bends. This man who called out to her as though her rightful place was by his bedside might have to pay for Jolene's crimes with his life.

And if the man was dying, could she really let him take his last breaths alone? She figured not and jumped to her feet to approach his doorway. He sat up in his bed, looking ready to rip out his IV. "Yes," she told him. "I'm still here. Have you told Sheriff Matthews all you know about

Jolene? Do you know how we can find her?" She couldn't let the guy die before he spilled everything he knew.

The man fell back onto his bed, exhausted. The bends could wipe a person out. She wanted to be sympathetic, but the shooter was getting away.

"You're still alive. Thank God," he said, then searched her face from where his head rested on the pillow. "Have you been treated for your cuts? Are you well?"

"I'm fine." She cringed at the abrasiveness of her voice in comparison to his, but Gage Fontaine had no reason to care about her at all. No one did, and that was fine with her.

Rachelle caught the look of pity on Sheriff Owen Matthews's face. He stood at the bottom of the bed, his hand at his belt and wearing the same expression the islanders did when they looked at her. She supposed she couldn't blame him. After all, it was his wife who was the witness to her father's killing. The sheriff's wife, Miriam, almost became her father's next victim because of it. He should be looking at her with more than pity.

He should be looking at her with hatred.

Rachelle dropped her gaze to the floor, not able to take his stare any longer. After a second, she regrouped and looked back to Gage to get her answers. "How can we find Jolene?"

"Please, Rachelle, you can't go anywhere near her. Promise me you won't."

"Why? What's it to you?"

"Yes, Fontaine," Sheriff Matthews interjected. "Please explain yourself. What's your connection to this woman? A relationship gone bad? Why did she try to kill you and Rachelle?"

"Her name is Jolene Almed. She's a modern-day pirate who hijacks boats for her living, or more appropriately, for her boss who has it out for me. She must've followed me from my last port."

"And where was that?"

"Vietnam. Ca Mau Province. I'm a wreck diver and salvager."

"You mean treasure hunter."

"Call it what you want."

"How about I call it like I see it? You're nothing but a scavenger, looking to get rich any way you can. You don't care who gets hurt in the process. Isn't that right, Fontaine?"

Gage's face went slack, devoid of expression. Rachelle stepped up to intervene. This interrogation didn't feel right. Jolene was the one getting away. "Can we do this later, Owen? After you've searched the water surrounding the island for this pirate?"

Sheriff Matthews shook his head. "And what if Mr. Fontaine here dies before I get back? We don't have any information about who this woman is. Or who he is." Owen Matthews faced Gage again. "Fontaine, while you have breath in you, you'd better start talking. I have an island to protect, and I want to know if you've brought danger to its shores. I'm going to need to know now."

Gage blinked and looked over at her. He sighed and his blue eyes softened. With a nod, he said, "I'm sorry, but yes. I've brought danger to Stepping Stones. And to you, Rachelle. I should have known Jolene was following me. She wanted my yacht, and wouldn't stop until she got it. But in the process, you got in the way. If she thinks you can identify her, she won't stop until that's been resolved."

"You mean until Rachelle has been killed?" Sheriff Matthews verified.

Rachelle heard her air rush out from her lungs. Was this conversation really going in this direction? Was it really happening at all? By the men's hard, serious faces, it seemed so. Rachelle crossed her arms at her chest. "You can't be serious. I was just doing my job. I wasn't bothering anyone, and now I'm on someone's hit list? What does this mean?"

"It means I keep you safe while I track this woman down," Owen said.

"There's no way you can watch Rachelle and work. Let me help," Gage implored. "It's my fault Jolene is here."

"Which is why I'm going to say no. I don't trust you either, Fontaine. If that's even your real name. You can guarantee I'll be looking to find out. I'm a former DEA agent. I know how to sniff the bad guys out, and if you're one, you'll wish you never came treasure hunting on my shores." Owen turned and stepped past her for the door. "Let's go, Rachelle. I'm taking you to your uncle's home. That's the safest place for you right now."

"No." She pinched her lips and halted him. She wanted nothing from anyone. "I'm twenty-six years old. I can take care of myself." She angled her head to see him staring her down. It didn't matter. She wouldn't change her mind.

"I don't want you staying alone at your house, but we'll talk about this when I get back from searching the waters. Until then you're not to go out to sea alone. Something tells me these are people who know how to make you disappear." Owen looked back at Gage. "Don't leave the island, Fontaine. I'm not through with you yet." With that he walked out.

Rachelle dropped her folded arms to her waist and looked everywhere but at Gage. She didn't trust him, either, but he was someone who didn't know anything about her, and for that reason, she felt more comfortable with him than anyone else at the moment.

"He's right, you know. You shouldn't go to sea alone, if at all right now. It's not safe."

"I can't stay here. I'll go crazy." She averted her gaze to the window, wanting to keep him in the dark about her family for a little while longer. "I just have to."

"The sea's in your blood, is it? I understand. I feel the same way."

She forced a smile, letting him believe that's what kept her off the land. It wouldn't be long before one of the islanders told him the truth. She'd take the anonymity for however long she could.

The fact was the sea and her blood didn't mix. The view from her boat of the eerie, endless expanse of the dark water all around her sometimes brought on a little panic, but after this past year, staying on land made her feel worse. The idea of being grounded now was a no-go. "Do I really need to be concerned for my safety from this woman?"

"Yes, you do." Gage sat up, the sheet dropping a bit to his waistline. He wore a green scrub shirt, but she couldn't miss the strength he had in his torso. He was one strong man, and with his black hair brushing against his neck and his facial growth, he looked a bit wild. Almost like a pirate himself.

Maybe he was.

"Rachelle, I'm going to ask you to please not leave here without me. I know how these people play."

"These people? You mean there's more than one I have to worry about?"

Gage hesitated but then shook his head. "Not right now. Right now I believe it's just Jolene, but that's enough. Promise me you'll take this seriously."

Rachelle chewed on the inside of her cheek for a few seconds. "Only if you tell me why you're on Stepping

Stones. You're a treasure hunter. There's no treasure around here."

He eyed her crossed arms and smirked. "I'm sure no one has ever dared to tell you this, *mi joya,* but you're wrong. There's a whole collection of gold and silver right out that window." He nodded to indicate the sea behind her. "And it's my job to find it."

My jewel? She nearly sputtered at the meaning of the delicate Spanish words he called her. There was nothing delicate about her, and he was about to find out. "Why is it your job? Who do you work for?"

"I work for myself, but I partner with a group of marine archaeologists. I research and scout out possible wrecks for them. The ocean is filled with them. More than three million to be exact, and most of these sunken boats didn't go down empty. The ship I'm tracking here is the *Maria's Joy.* She was an eighteenth-century galleon out of Spain. Her manifest documents state she took down millions in gold and silver."

"What was she doing in the North Atlantic?" Rachelle held up her hand as an absurd thought crossed her mind. "Wait…" She paused to think her crazy idea through. Could Gage's presence here really be about the pirates who used to live on Stepping Stones back in the eighteenth century? "Don't even tell me this has something to do with Pirate Island."

"So you know your history." He grinned wide, showing a perfect smile that nearly caused her knees to buckle.

But Rachelle would never be so weak. She ignored the effects his smile had on her by imagining the flash of a gold tooth among his straight, white teeth. It allowed her to remember not to fall for the seaman's suave demeanor. She wondered if she was the first not to cave. Judging by his charming good looks and his rich lifestyle on his expensive yacht, she doubted anyone had ever told the man no.

She wouldn't let that stop her. With arms crossed at her chest, she said, "I know my history enough to know the only traces left by the pirates who used to live on Stepping Stones are the empty caverns carved into the cliffs. No treasure was left in them or anywhere on the island. You're wasting your time. The only treasure you should be chasing right now is that beautiful boat of yours. But then, you probably plan to buy a bigger and better one, anyway, so why should you care if someone makes off with this one? You were probably born with *ten* silver spoons in your mouth. Must be nice to live so freely."

His smile faded. "Freely? No, I don't live freely. I have plenty of people who want to take my freedom away. One in particular is Jolene, which is why I need you to promise me you will not go out there alone."

Her answer came swiftly as she mimicked his earlier words to her. "I'm sure no one has ever dared to tell you this, my treasure hunter friend, but no. I will not make that promise. And if you won't help me track this pirate, then I will go alone. I will not allow her to escape justice."

"Even if that means you never come back to shore?" His blue eyes flashed to prove his point. "Because that's how she'll make it look. Like you've been lost at sea. No one will ever see you again."

Rachelle shrugged and scoffed, "I'm already lost. No one's missed me yet." On the heel of her rubber boots, she turned with a squeak and left Gage and his quizzical expression behind.

Gage opened his eyes. Moonlight streamed in through the edge of the blinds casting shadows across his room. He looked to his right for the time, but his red-numbered clock wasn't there. He shot up and felt the pain in his arm. At his grab he remembered he'd been cut. Realization of where he was settled over him. The clinic on Stepping Stones. Not his yacht. His yacht was gone.

For now.

He would get it back, he silently vowed. This fight wasn't over yet. He doubted it would ever be over. Marcus was a lethal pirate boss. The only thing worse was a lethal pirate boss with vengeance on his mind.

Vengeance and the means to carry it out.

A rustling sound came from outside Gage's open door. The night nurse probably doing paperwork. Gage settled back down, sinking into his pillow with eyes closed. He concentrated on the decompressed parts of his body, curling his toes tight. No pain in his legs shot up. He took that as a good prognosis. He was on the mend. It wouldn't take forty-eight hours to break out of here after all. The Lord knew he didn't have forty-eight hours.

Gage made a mental plan: Leave here in the morning, find Jolene, and run her far away from here. She was a nuisance he couldn't have here, and not because she was a threat to him, but because where one pirate showed up, another would follow shortly after.

And Marcus was something to fear.

The rustling sound came again from the waiting room. Gage's eyes opened to the noise and he peered at the door. It sounded like someone shifting on vinyl. He remembered Rachelle had at least promised to stay the night. Without her boat, she wouldn't get far anyway. The rustling noise had to be her tossing and turning out on the couch. It probably wasn't very comfortable, but she'd said it was better than staying at her uncle's house, for whatever reason. Gage was just glad he'd convinced her not to go to her cottage down by the shore. Living alone wouldn't be safe for her until he convinced Jolene to leave.

Even then, he wouldn't be able to keep Jolene at bay for very long. But once he located the *Maria's Joy* and her treasure, he could use some of his take to bargain with her to leave Rachelle alone. Money talks. Especially gold and silver.

And a lot of gold and silver, according to the galleon's manifest that documented its cargo when it set sail in 1726. Gage's research showed pirates captured the ship before its precious goods were ever unloaded and sank it in and around Stepping Stones. Or "Pirate Island" as Rachelle called it. The island was dubbed the name for its plundering residents at the time, a group of vile criminals who even warred amongst each other for dominion over the island.

Gage had to admit that after seeing the island in person, he understood the lure to control such an isolated and protected piece of land. Stepping Stones had to be at least a two-hour boat ride from the mainland in today's power-motor standards. In the early 1700s, no one was getting anywhere near here without warning. And even if they did, huge flat, and nearly submerged rocks surrounded the island. A natural barricade to keep enemies away. Large boats would have a hard time getting anywhere near the island, back then and today. Gage's boat included.

He sighed and punched the bed beside him. He needed his boat. His whole life was on the *Getaway*. But most importantly, all his maps and documents and research needed to find the *Maria's Joy* was on there, too. Without it, he would never find the treasure. He learned a long time ago, the sea didn't give her secrets up to anyone. It didn't matter whose side you were on.

A muffled screech broke into his thoughts. The sound

came from the waiting room, and he tuned his ear in time to hear it again. Was Rachelle having a nightmare?

Or living one?

Gage jumped from his bed at lightning speed and tore the IV from his arm. Pain ripped through him, but he used it to propel him faster out the door, just in time to see a masked man standing over Rachelle.

Or, most likely, a masked woman.

It had to be Jolene with one hand over Rachelle's mouth, the other gripping a syringe with its sharp point up and aimed right for Rachelle's neck.

Gage made a dash for Jolene's wrist, swinging her around and away from Rachelle. Twisting her wrist, he managed to change the direction of the needle onto Jolene. She grabbed at his wrist with her other hand and fought back with a brutal force. He always knew she was strong. She'd have to be, with the felonious company she kept. They ate their own.

He knew this, having been one of them.

"You want to be first? Fine," she gritted out through her teeth. The needle pointing at her chest barely fazed her.

"Where's my boat, Jolene?" He had to know before things got worse for her, but even as he asked, Gage moved his thumb up to reach the plunger of the syringe. If he could empty it, no one would be dying tonight.

"It's not your boat. It never was." She threw her words into his face as her eyes glared through the slits of her mask.

His thumb inched closer to the plunger as the two of them sweated in their battle of wills and strength. The syringe moved toward him, then back on her. Finally his thumb found its mark, and in one quick push, the clear liquid shot up and over Jolene's shoulder.

She screamed her frustration. "Twelve hours," she said,

pushing Gage back. "Then I make a phone call. Give the treasure and yourself up, or you know who will have to pay you a visit. As for her—" Jolene jerked her head in Rachelle's direction "—she's dead either way." The masked woman ran to the front doors and burst through, becoming a shadow in the dark night.

Gage didn't have to ask who she would be calling. He knew the answer already.

Marcus.

"You're just going to let her go?" Rachelle jumped to her feet and ran to the night nurse, who was moaning on the floor by her desk. Jolene had apparently knocked her out. Rachelle picked up the phone to dial out a number.

"Who are you calling?" Gage stepped up to help the confused nurse into a sitting position.

"Sheriff Matthews. Maybe he can stop her before she gets too far. She needs to be caught. Before someone else has to pay for her crimes."

"The only person that will end up paying for this will be you."

"Nothing new there."

Gage shook his head, unable to fathom the meaning of her words as well as her earlier comment about already being lost. The only thing he knew was that Rachelle was in greater danger than he'd thought. It was going to take a lot more to get Jolene to leave now. More than a cut in the profits. More than a boat. If she made that phone call in twelve hours, it would most likely a cost a life.

His.

THREE

The clinic's fluorescent lighting beamed bright, while the world outside remained dark and oblivious to the malicious presence on the island. Dr. Schaffer had returned and comforted poor Ruby. The night nurse's sobs echoed through the room while he checked her vitals. Her wails really peaked to their crescendo when Sheriff Matthews came through the door.

"How's Ruby?" Owen asked the doctor.

"Her vitals are good. But she has a nasty bump on the head that I'll keep an eye on. I think she'll be fine, though."

"I'm sorry, Ruby." Owen frowned. "With only me and one deputy on the island, covering every square inch is impossible. But I promise, I'll be calling in some reinforcements so this doesn't happen again."

Owen hunkered down and, with gloves, scooped up and inspected an empty injection vile. He read the label on the bottle and lifted angry eyes at Rachelle. He didn't need to say anything for her to know it was something lethal. He probably knew all about deadly drugs from his past work in the Drug Enforcement Agency. In jerky movements, he bagged the evidence along with the syringe Jolene left behind, then stood. Prints would be processed, but so what? If Jolene didn't want to be found, she wouldn't be. And once she left the vicinity and surrounding waters, she'd be out of his jurisdiction.

Gage came out of his room, a pair of black jeans swapped out for the scrubs he'd worn before. His wet suit was in his hand.

"Going somewhere?" Owen asked him.

"I thought I'd get a jump on the day. Thank you, Dr. Schaffer, for leaving me the pants. Just put them on my bill. Now, if you'll excuse me, I have a boat to track, and I'm sure when I find it, I'll find Jolene."

"Or set sail on the *Getaway*. Isn't that what you call your boat? Seems fitting for a thief."

"I didn't name her. The previous owner did and not for the reasons you believe. Not that it's any of your business." Gage looked past Owen and grabbed Rachelle's attention with his piercing blue eyes. "Rachelle, I need to speak with you for a moment. Do you mind?"

She hesitated for a second but stood and followed him into his room. Or old room since the sheets were already removed and bunched in a ball on the floor. "Checking out already? Is that safe?"

He grunted. "Safer than staying here. This place isn't exactly safeguarded as we found out tonight."

"I mean about your sickness. Is it safe for you to leave yet? How do you feel?" She studied his face for signs of his illness, but at his smirk, she looked toward the bed instead.

"Thank you for your concern, but I've been around enough people with the bends, even watched someone die once—" He swallowed so hard she heard his gulp and looked back at him. "Anyway, I'm on the mend. I feel all right, but honestly, I would feel even better knowing you're in a safe place. Would you please consider going to your uncle's?"

"Absolutely not." She lifted her chin.

"How about a friend's house then?"

Rachelle felt her lips twitch. She shook her head, unable to say she had no friends. Her best friend, Gretchen, hadn't spoken to her in eleven months.

"How about your parents? Where are they? Do they live on the mainland? Can you go to them?"

"My mom lives here, but I can't stay there. I feel uncomfortable there."

He closed in to within a foot of her. "Uncomfortable? You're going to be dead if you don't go someplace safe. Comfort doesn't matter right now. Jolene works for a pirate boss who spends his days ordering hijacks on the Mediterranean Sea for ransom. People who don't comply are killed. These hijackers carry Uzis and use them regularly—as you well know, having been on the receiving end of one. There are hijacks going on right now as we speak, with hostages held at gunpoint with no one to come to their aid. If you're American, maybe the Navy's Special Ops will come in to negotiate for you. But even that doesn't always end well. Modern-day piracy is real. And if I don't chase Jolene away from here, that boss I mentioned will be on your shores tomorrow. *That* should be the only thing that makes you uncomfortable."

It did, but she hoped it didn't show.

"Take me to your mom's house, so I can see if it's something I can work with to keep you safe. One bonus is Jolene won't know to look for you there right away. She'll probably look for your house first." Gage waved an arm for her to lead the way.

She didn't budge.

"Now what's wrong?"

"You can't go to my mom's house. No one goes to my mom's house." She raised her chin again, but this time it was not in indignation, but rather to look him in the eyes and plead with him. "Ever."

Never had Gage been able to say no to emeralds, and looking into Rachelle's bright green eyes, he nearly agreed to stay out of her mother's house—or rather a better name for the building would be a neglected structure with easy break-in capabilities. For that reason, he'd be staying with her here, no matter how bright her eyes shined when she asked him to stay out.

"I'm coming in with you." He trod carefully on the wooden porch as it cracked beneath him. He also couldn't miss the way the porch came away from the house. Would it hold under his weight? Gage looked back at Rachelle. "No negotiating. This place isn't exactly what I'd call secure." The wood cracked again as if on cue. "Or safe."

Rachelle's lips frowned. "My mom isn't very handy. Since my dad left last year, she's kind of…hit rock bottom."

"Been there," he mumbled, but opened the screened door without any further elaboration. The screen flapped in his face where a tear sliced up the middle. Had Jolene already been here? he wondered, as he touched the screen. Would he find her waiting for them inside? The woman was clever. After all, she had stowed away on his yacht waiting for her most opportune moment to catch him beneath the sea. "Was this screen cut before, or is the slice new?" He asked and looked over his shoulder to catch the roll of Rachelle's eyes.

"About a year ago. Some teenagers thought they were being cool."

"Vandalism isn't cool."

Rachelle shrugged. "Doesn't matter. They got away with it." Her face was a mask of indifference morphed as their eyes locked. She wore the guise often. He wondered what her true feelings were and why she covered them up. She pushed past him and severed their connection before he could ask.

"Hold your nose," she instructed, and turned the doorknob. With that, she pushed the door wide and the room released a pungent, sweet odor. "Mom, it's me, Rachelle," she called at the door, with her hands still on the doorknob. "I'm coming in, and I have company with me." She angled her head to view him over her shoulder. "You're looking green."

Gage did his best not to cringe, especially when Rachelle walked into the house with ease. As she scanned the empty living room, he whispered behind her, "What is that smell?"

She walked to the foot of the stairs. Her hand brushed the dusty railing, then came away to wipe her fingertips across her blue jeans. "I bring her food, but she doesn't eat it. It ends up rotting. I haven't been here in weeks, and as you can see, I can't stay here now. And not just because of the lack of security. I'll be right back. I just want to check on her upstairs, then we can get out of here."

He watched her ascend the staircase with rigid grace. Her body exuded strength that surpassed muscle power and edged into an emotional and mental poise that came with experience. Something wasn't right in Rachelle's childhood home, and she'd been toughened up because of it.

Gage had his own toughening-up experience as a child who grew up in the foster-care system, never having a solid place to call home. He had to wonder, though, if no home was better than Rachelle's home.

This place didn't feel like it toughened her up, but instead, beat her down. It was a fine line that just might explain her mask of indifference.

She disappeared above and as he heard her open and close a door, he swept his finger across a foyer table with an inch of dust. The piece of furniture actually looked like an antique, and after a quick perusal through the adjacent living room, he thought all the furniture was expensive under its filth.

Things hadn't always been bad in the home. So what happened to Rachelle's family?

"Who are you?" A voice yanked him around. An older, messy version of Rachelle stood in front of him. The woman's raven hair had streaks of gray threading through it, and she would probably be striking if it was combed and styled.

"I'm—I'm Gage." He whipped out his hand to shake, but her dull, emotionless eyes didn't notice. He tucked his hand back to his side. "I'm here with Rachelle. She's upstairs. I think she's looking for you. You're her mom, right?"

No reply. He wasn't sure she even heard him.

"I'm sorry, I didn't mean to intrude—"

"I used to be." Her monotone voice cut him off. Gage floundered for the meaning of her words. He wasn't following.

"You used to be…what?" He leaned forward to bring his face to her level. She wasn't a really short woman, but the way she held herself, hunched her body over and down a few inches.

"Her mom." She pulled at her snarled, greasy hair. "I wasn't a good mom." She turned to the stairs. "Take her out of here and don't let her come back. It's best this way." The woman shuffled up the stairs, disappearing from view.

From above, Rachelle called out, "There you are, Mom. I was looking for you. Do you want me to make you something to eat? It's no trouble. Really. How about some eggs? Did you eat the eggs I brought you?"

With each of her questions, Gage heard no reply from

the other woman. Rachelle's one-sided conversation wrenched at his heart. She was trying to reach her mother somewhere under the covering of some kind of pain. He wondered how long this had been going on and leaned forward to hear more of the conversation, but the bedroom door closed with a soft click and Rachelle's firm footsteps neared the top of the staircase. At the sound of her feet on the stairs, Gage grabbed a magazine off the coffee table to look busy. He had to wipe the dust off to read the title. The date caught his attention first. It was a little over a year ago, and he had to think it made total sense. It was as though the whole house, inhabitant included, stopped living on that date.

"Let's go," Rachelle said from the foyer, racing to the front door without looking his way.

Gage tossed the magazine and suppressed the cough that the forming dust cloud caused. "I met your mom."

She halted with her hand on the doorknob. Her gaze dropped to the gray Persian rug that he was pretty sure used to be blue and yellow. "She never used to be like this. I mean, sometimes she had little bouts of depression," Rachelle hushed her tone, causing him to hold his breath and step toward her to hear her. "But she always came back. I don't think she's coming back this time."

As much as he wanted to place a comforting hand on Rachelle's shoulder, she looked as if she would fracture into a million pieces if he did. Gage curled his hands as he reached her at the door. "From that rock bottom you mentioned before," he said with a low voice.

She nodded while she pressed her tight lips.

"Rachelle, have you prayed for your mom?"

Her eyes flashed and her hard, shell exterior reformed around her. With the lift of her chin and her snide voice back in place, she said, "God doesn't care about my prayers."

"Why do you think that?"

She shrugged. "I have too much of my father in me."

"Is that a bad thing?" Gage did wonder what role Mr. Thibodaux played in the mess surrounding him.

"Well, it sure doesn't earn me any Brownie points."

"Where is your dad? He's obviously not around. Was he a deadbeat?"

Rachelle shook her head, and her silky raven hair like her mom's, except without the streaks, fell gracefully past her shoulders. Her lips remained closed.

"Is it safe for you to stay with him?"

Another flash of something he couldn't decipher filled her eyes. "He's in prison," she answered quickly. "No, I can't stay with him. Nor would I want to."

The words *for what?* sat on the tip of Gage's tongue, but if Rachelle wanted to tell him, she would. And it really didn't matter what her old man had done. The only thing that mattered was finding a safe place for her now. "Okay, so your dad is out. Can you think of any other place Jolene wouldn't find you? I'd say the mainland, but I don't think there's enough time."

"The tunnels. They were carved into the cliffs back when piracy here was real."

"Hate to tell you this, but it is again. The tunnels sound promising, though. Where are they located?"

"There are a few caverns in different places on the island, but there's one with an entrance below my uncle's restaurant that I could break into."

"Break into? I wouldn't want you to get into any trouble."

She shrugged her tight shoulders. "It wouldn't shock anyone more than they already have been."

"Because of your father?"

Rachelle nodded and looked past him out the smudged windows facing Main Street.

Gage itched to pull this broken young woman into his arms and give her a hug. Instead, he sighed and said, "Regardless of what you think, Rachelle, God does care about your prayers. He also cares about you no matter how much of your father you think you have in you. Trust me. He knows about your rock bottom, and He cares. I know because He rescued me from some pretty deep waters, and I didn't have anyone else's sin in me. All that bad in me was all me, and He still rescued me."

She remained quiet for a minute and studied him with pinched lips, then said, "Must be nice." She pulled the door wide and stepped out without looking back. "Careful on the front steps. We haven't been rescued, like yourself."

"Actually," he said as he followed her out the door, "if you don't mind, I'd like to come back later and see about fixing these. Regardless of all those silver spoons you think were shoved in my mouth when I was born, I'm pretty handy with a hammer and nails. It shouldn't take more than a couple hours."

Rachelle squinted, her lips curled in suspicion. "Why?"

"Because I'm a fast worker."

"No, I mean why do you care?"

He shrugged his shoulder less than an inch. "Because, like I said, my little sharp-tongued skeptic, I know what it feels like to hit rock bottom. Or, in my case, drown in deep waters."

She lifted her dainty chin, but there was nothing dainty about the edge in her words. "Unless you were the one drowning someone else, we have nothing in common."

He knew she was trying to show how bad she thought

she was. But nothing she could say would shock him. Not when his past actions were a whole lot worse.

He stepped up to her, their toes practically touching. She came to his chin, but he leaned forward as he had with her mom. Gage met Rachelle at eye level and hooked her full attention. "Who said I didn't drown someone?"

FOUR

Gage Fontaine was a killer? Rachelle removed the key ring from her jeans pocket and threaded the longest and sharpest key to protrude through her fingers. It wouldn't be much of a weapon against him if he tried something down in the caverns, but she had the element of knowledge on her side. She knew her way through every twist and turn of the blown-out and carved-out tunnel, starting from the cellar of the Blue Lobster to where the tunnel opened out to the cove on the other side of the cliff.

"Where is everyone?" Gage asked from behind as they entered the empty restaurant through the side kitchen entrance.

She flipped a light switch and illuminated the stainless-steel room with fluorescent lighting. "The Blue Lobster's only open for dinner. When I worked here, I would open it for lunch, but..."

"But you enjoy catching the buggers instead of serving them?"

She didn't respond as she pushed through the swinging door to the dining room. The lighting in there cast more of a candlelit effect with sconces on the walls. Sconces that accented the framed photos above them.

Rachelle was surprised to still see the pictures hanging

where she'd positioned them years ago. Wouldn't Uncle Jerome want to be rid of anything that reminded him of his brother? Wasn't that why he offered her the job of going out to sea? To be rid of her?

"Great photographs." Gage stepped up to one of the frames. "What kind of bird is this?"

"It's a snowy egret."

"He's cool. I like his spiked hairdo." Gage flashed his wide grin, showcasing laugh lines as deep as his voice. Laughing blue eyes that told the story of his joyful life. Must be nice. She looked away. "Did someone on the island take all these?"

"Yeah." She shifted her weight from one foot to the other. "I did."

"You?" He crossed his arms and moved to another photo. He peered closely at a photograph of a red-tailed hawk she'd taken three years ago. She could tell Gage's attention went straight to the bird's golden brown eyes. That had been the goal when she'd purposely blurred the background of green trees and blue sky just enough to put the focus on the bird's face. Normally, she would have underexposed the image to saturate all the colors, but she wanted the detail in the eyes and beak to dominate the photo. "He's an amazing creature." Gage still kept his gaze locked on the photo. "Beautiful doesn't describe it. With his beak open to show his tongue so clearly, I feel like he's about to swoop down to catch his food or me. But it's the eyes that grab you. It's like…"

"It's like they tell you their story."

"Yes. You must have some lens on your camera to get this close." He looked around at her for the first time, but it wasn't for long. A few beats, and the hawk pulled his attention back.

She hummed while she tried to remember what equipment she used. "I think I shot him at 300mm. Wildlife photography requires more of a reach, especially for birds high up in their nests like this one. I got as close as I could without endangering myself, but it was still a harrowing experience."

Gage swung back around, this time his attention focused only on her, birds forgotten. "I'm glad to hear safety ranks high for you, but there are other creatures of prey out there that are more dangerous than this guy. I don't want you taking any more harrowing risks."

"Not even for a good shot? Because when I snapped Jolene's photo, I made sure to zoom in on her face for a clear ID. Her gray eyes glaring at me tell me her story real well. They say she's a thief."

Gage's mouth slackened in silence—but not for long. "Are you telling me you took Jolene's picture?" His eyes widened as another thought crossed his face. "Does she know?"

"Of course she knows. She looked right at me. I was hoping she would smile, but the only things she showered me with were bullets."

Gage rubbed at his forehead as he muttered aloud, "No wonder Jolene wants you dead. You can do more than describe her. You have a photo of her."

"Many of them, actually. And all catching her in the act."

"Where's the camera now?"

"Why? So you can hand it over to her? No way. She is going down for her crimes before someone else has to pay for them."

"Or, *you* pay with your life, and she gets the camera anyway."

"Doesn't matter if she gets her hands on it now. I gave it to Sheriff Matthews as soon as we got back to land. I'm

sure he's made copies by now. I hope he has, anyway."
Rachelle crossed her arms and shook her head. "The man
seems more determined to get something on you, instead
of going after a criminal." Rachelle eyed Gage. She pursed
her lips and speculated aloud. "But then, maybe he *should*
be looking into who you are. After all, you did say you
drowned someone before. Maybe you belong behind bars
with Jolene. Maybe you're on the lam, as well? Is that why
you call your boat the *Getaway?* You're running from the
law? Who did you kill? What's your story, Gage?"

Gage lifted his hands up. "Whoa, Sherlock, before you
have me drawn and quartered, why don't we sit down."
He waved for her to have a seat at one of the many dining room tables.

Rachelle didn't budge.

"I promise to tell you everything."

"All I want to know is if you killed someone."

"It's not that easy."

"It is to me. You either did or you didn't."

Gage sighed and went to the table alone. He pulled out
a chair and sat. At her nod, he began, "I didn't mean to."

Rachelle headed to the exit.

"Wait! Rachelle, please, hear me out first. If not for me,
then at least for your own safety. You can't be out there
alone while Jolene is slinking around the island. Please.
Don't go."

Rachelle made it to the front entrance and held the
iron door handle, ready to open the heavy oak door to the
boardwalk. It wasn't Gage's plea that stopped her, though.
Through the small window, she could see a lot of people walking by. Her first thought was to shield her face
with something. Maybe the potted roses by the door. She
reached for the pot, then saw Gretchen walk by, hand in
hand with her deputy boyfriend.

Rachelle shrunk back from the window, hoping her former best friend didn't see her staring out the window.

Gretchen walked by with her long, blond curls brushing against her high school sweetheart's shoulder. Gretchen was all light compared to Rachelle's dark. A point driven home more now than ever. Two friends, complete opposites in everything. Billy Baker tugged Gretchen's hand where they were linked and pulled her pale complexioned face closer to his. They shared something funny and intimate. Something that caused Gretchen to look adoringly up at her man with her annoyingly perfect and sweet smile.

Rachelle stepped back from the door, unable to witness their happiness any longer. Not that she faulted Gretchen for it. Why shouldn't she be happy? Gretchen's dad hadn't killed anyone. Her life wasn't destroyed. So what if she lost a friend. She had her other friends, and she had her boyfriend.

"Thank you for staying." Gage's voice seeped into Rachelle's biting thoughts. "Like I said, I didn't mean to cause Pete's death."

"Pete?" she murmured, trying to remember what they had been talking about.

"The captain of the *Getaway,* Pete Masters. The man who died."

She nodded and looked back at the door. Leaving through it didn't feel like the best choice now. Even though the alternative was to stay with a killer.

"He taught me everything I know about diving," Gage continued. "When I was seventeen, I was on a road to worse than nowhere. I was on a road to a bottomless pit where the worst scavengers took what they wanted and left nothing but bones behind. It was Pete who saved me. He pulled me up from that heinous place. And how did I repay him?" Gage gave a bitter laugh that brought Rachelle back fully to what this stranger was offering her.

His deepest, darkest secrets.

Why?

For him to spill his dark secrets, he must really want her to trust him. Need her to even. For her own safety, as he'd said? Or for something more personal?

Rachelle stepped toward the table not sure why she did. Maybe because Gage was all dark like herself. Maybe she recognized the misery as the same that coursed through her.

And since when did misery turn away company?

"Okay, I'll bite." She grabbed a chair and sat down across from him. She rested her arms on the thick veneered oak table and leaned in. "How did Pete die?"

"Decompression sickness. He died within thirty minutes of resurfacing. I pulled him out of the water already unconscious, but he never regained consciousness."

"The bends?" she said with confusion. "How does that make it your fault?"

"He used my equipment. I handed him my tank, thinking it was full." Gage shook his head and locked his gaze to where Rachelle fiddled with a rolled-up blue napkin. "I always refilled my tanks after use. But I must not have this time. It was near empty, and Pete had to rush to the surface, and…"

"And?"

"Nothing. That's it. End of story. Pete died. I handed him an empty tank, and I killed him."

"But you didn't mean it?"

"Does it matter? He's still dead because of me. After everything he did for me."

"You said that before. What exactly did he do for you?"

Gage huffed. "Are you ready for this?"

"Can't surprise me, but go ahead and try."

"I grew up jumping from one foster home to another. Can honestly say I never had a home, and when I was seventeen, I ran away and ended up at a big freight port in Jersey. That's where I met the scavengers I mentioned. They were eyeing their next hijack, and I was looking to belong."

"Is this where you met Jolene?"

Gage nodded. "She was the leader of the group."

"So you were a pirate." Rachelle removed her arms from the table and leaned back in her chair. That door was seeming like the safer choice by the second. Even if Gretchen was still out there.

"I would have been if I'd passed their first test."

"And what was that?"

"Simple. Kill the captain of the *Getaway,* and steal the yacht for Jolene's boss."

"Boss?"

Gage barely nodded. His response was more of a tick in his jaw. "More like a warlord. His name is Marcus. I've never actually met him, but Pete told me all about him. Every despicable thing he's done on the water, and off, all in the name of money."

"Did Pete tell you what he looked like?"

"Only that he's bald with a tattoo on the back of his head. Not too many people have actually seen him or the tattoo and lived to tell what either looks like, but Pete believed it to be the letter *P* with a sword cut through it. The pirate warlord doesn't typically turn his back on his enemies, or his friends, I'm sure. It doesn't matter for me, though. I figure he'll be gloating and announcing himself the day he finally catches up to me…right before he kills me."

Rachelle's stomach clenched with the visual of a gleeful pirate standing over Gage, but she cleared her throat and pushed on for more, much needed information. She would need it before making a judgment call about Gage and his innocence. "What was the bad blood between Pete and him? Why did he want your friend dead?"

"Pete had infiltrated some of Marcus's biggest boat thefts when he was in the navy."

"Pete had?"

"He was a retired navy captain, special ops. Ambushed many hijacks all over the world. Some were Marcus's. I had no idea there was history between them, and when Jolene gave the order to steal the *Getaway,* she was really giving *me* a death sentence. She knew what Pete had been trained to do in the navy. She wasn't about to take him on, but why not order the pirate wannabe to do it? She sent me in to fight to someone's death, but neglected to tell me it most likely would be my own." Gage smirked, and his eyes actually lit up. "The laugh was on me, I guess. Ha-ha." He flashed his big smile at her.

Rachelle couldn't see what was so funny about the situation, but this strange man sitting across from her seemed to walk around life with this naive idea that the world was one rosebush after another. "How is this funny?" she asked.

"Believe me, it *wasn't* funny that night. Pete took me down before I had both feet on his deck. I rowed out to where his boat was anchored and was flat on my back the second I boarded. I knew right away Jolene set me up. I fought back real hard, and thought if I could kill Pete first, I could take the boat for myself, but after Pete's skilled blows, I knew that was wishful thinking, and I was the only one dying that night."

"But you're still alive. What happened?"

Gage stopped smiling. His eyes dimmed and misted a bit. The swift change from the jolly pirate to one full of woe made him even more hard to read. She didn't know which one she liked better.

Or which one was real.

"God happened. Remember that rock bottom I mentioned at your mom's house? I was swimming with the scavengers, ready to kill someone for them for no reason. But I was rescued that night. Pulled out of that pit by my Savior. Not a day goes by that I don't say 'Thank You, Jesus' for using Pete to lift me out of that dark place. Because Pete was obedient to God that night, I am alive today. When Pete could have delivered his final death blow, he offered me a new life instead, one with Christ at the helm and a friend by my side."

"Well, you must not be as bad as you think then. God doesn't bother with those who are a lost cause."

"Wrong. We're all lost and need a Savior to get us home. But we have to be willing to say yes. That's the only thing I did right that night. When Pete offered me his hand, I didn't have to take it. But I said yes, and God met me right there and saved me."

"Except, you're still being chased down by Jolene and her warlord boss man. Why?"

Gage shrugged. "Retaliation. Marcus doesn't like being bested. I set sail that night on the boat he wanted. He won't stop until he gets it. It's a matter of principle now."

"Correct me if I'm wrong, but did God really save you then? Or did He just give you a life of being chased by your past? No offense, but I'll keep my lost life. At least this way, my past can't chase me down if I accept it as my lot in life."

Gage grew quiet. He stood and went to the front bay window. Beyond the boardwalk and beyond the pier, the ocean expanded out to a blur on the horizon. Waves rolled into shore with a strength that indicated a storm brewed farther out than the eye could see, but Rachelle had to wonder if more turmoil raged inside the Blue Lobster than outside. Had her words brought something up to the surface in Gage? Something he didn't want to face?

"How long have you been running, Gage?"

"Fifteen years."

"That's a long time. Aren't you tired?"

He kept his back to her as he spoke. "God never promised an easy life, but He promised to be with us through it. But you know what, Rachelle? You might be on to something. Jesus also came to set me free from my past. That evil isn't me anymore, but maybe I've allowed the chase as a reminder of where I came from and what I've done. But if I truly believe I'm forgiven for all that, then I shouldn't have to spend the rest of my life looking over my shoulder at the evil chasing me—" he glanced over his shoulder "—and now chasing you, whether you want to believe it, or not. Maybe my time in Stepping Stones is more than just finding the final resting place of an old ship. Maybe Stepping Stones is where I break these chains, once and for all, and finally find peace."

"The only way you will find peace is by destroying these people before they destroy you."

His eyebrows nearly reach the ceiling. "So, it's kill or be killed? Is that what you're saying?"

Rachelle zipped her eyes to the wide-open sea. The shock in his eyes mirrored the shock expanding in her chest. Had she really said killing was the answer?

Yes. Yes, she had.

There *was* a beast in her. That's all there was to it. She could no longer presume she might be like her father. Now she had the proof.

Rachelle stood and headed to the door behind the hostess counter. It took three tries to insert the key into the lock. "Let's go if we're going," she said.

"Where?"

"To the tunnels. If anyone should be locked up, it should be me."

"Are you sure you're safe down here?" Gage asked from behind as they stepped carefully on a set of wooden stairs leading down into the chilled darkness of granite walls. "I can't believe this is all below your family's restaurant."

"I hate these caverns more than anything. They give me the creeps, but they're the best place to hide on the island. Very few people know where they exit, including many of the islanders."

"But you know where they lead?"

"Some are dead ends and were set up as traps, but this one used to connect up to another set of tunnels that lead to the shore and also to the sheriff's house. The previous owner of his house was good friends with my grandfather before they both passed on. Before my grandfather died, he blocked his tunnel off from the other."

"A falling-out between friends?"

"No. My grandfather learned his own son was using the tunnels for illegal purposes. He was stealing from him, so Grandpa locked them up tight."

"Sounds like a disappointing moment between father and son."

"The first of many before his son went to prison."

Her quick and bitter remark silenced Gage in the dim light from above. She'd said too much, but maybe it would be better if he heard the truth from her rather than an islander. Either way, it was only a matter of time.

"Let me guess," he said softly. "This son is your father."

She left the question hanging there and took a step out of the light. Breathing came easier in the dark.

"I'd say your grandfather wasn't the only one disappointed." Gage paused and looked above the stairs to the lit room that housed the wines for the restaurant. The Blue Lobster was a fine seafood establishment now owned by her uncle. But even though her grandfather left everything to him, she still worked hard to bring the freshest food to its tables, if only from her boat. "You lost your father and your job."

"When I worked here my favorite thing to do was to talk to everyone who came through the door. I would even sit down with them to hear about their day. Now, I can't face anyone. Me working at sea is best for everyone. Why make the customers uncomfortable by having the daughter of the island's convict wait on them?"

"What did he do, Rachelle? Why's he in prison?"

She looked away to the granite walls of the cavern as though Gage could see her. "It doesn't matter."

"It matters to you. Whatever he did bothers you. To the point you wear a mask of indifference, pretending you don't care."

Rachelle took another step deeper into the dark cavern, afraid of what else Gage would say about her. "I wear a what?" A cold wind pushed at her back, and she wrapped her arms around her chest.

"A mask. It keeps you going about your day. It keeps you alive like my diver's mask does for me. Without it, you would flounder and drown in the pain."

Rachelle backed up against the cold rock wall. More cold air lifted her hair. Her head faced the pressure of the wind.

Wind?

How could there be wind if the other end of the tunnel was boarded up and blocked off?

Unless it wasn't blocked off anymore.

"You can tell me, Rachelle. I won't hold his sins against you. I promise. You are not your father. You are Rachelle Thibodeaux, a beautiful person all in her own right."

"What?" she asked, trying to listen for any sounds from down the tunnel.

"All I'm saying is you're not an extension of your father. I know that's what you think of yourself. Did he kill someone? Is that what you're worried about? That you, too, could be capable of such a thing?"

The wind became forgotten. She nodded even though she knew he couldn't see her. Would he want more of an answer? Something that required her to speak up and give voice to the beast inside her?

He wouldn't think she was so beautiful then.

A chill ran up her spine, but at the lift of her hair, she had to think it was from more than the beast of a storm inside her. For wind to be passing through, the tunnel had to be open on the other end.

"Someone's in the tunnel," she announced.

In a spilt second, Gage stepped in front of her, his back to her to block her view from anyone. He stayed silent for a few seconds, then whispered, "You're right. The tunnel's open. Where does it end?"

"It links up to the sheriff's house, but it also forks off and ends in a cove on the other side of the cliff."

"That's got to be it. You're going to have to come with me. I can't leave you here now. Not if someone's in here."

Rachelle's hair lifted again on a breeze, then fell straight. The atmosphere tensed up in an instant, all wind cut off. "The door's shut," she whispered at Gage's back. He tensed and she realized her palms rested at his shoulders. When had she grabbed on? Didn't matter. She wasn't letting go anytime soon. "Do you think it's Jolene? Do you think she's in here?"

"Shh." His command barely made a sound. Gage slowly turned, and his arm came around and gave Rachelle a hard shove. "Run, now," he commanded through clenched teeth.

Run? To where? She had no flashlight. The caverns were completely dark. How could she run blindly into the dark? And what if Jolene was coming this way?

Gage gave her another push, but it was in the direction of the steps, not the tunnel. A bang, followed by crumbling rock falling on her head and shoulders nearly sent her to the ground. Rachelle's mind screamed, or maybe that was really her voice. Was someone shooting at them? Had they meant to hit the wall behind her, or had their shot missed its target.

Her.

"Run! Now!" Gage's third shove nearly toppled Rachelle, but this time she obeyed. Keeping her head tucked, she raced to the stairway and took the steps two at a time. When she reached the top, she expected Gage to be right behind her, but no one else came through the hatch.

Rachelle didn't want to shut the door, but she couldn't leave it open. What if the person came through? But then, if they wanted to get in, a flimsy lock wouldn't stop them. Not with the gun they toted.

"Gage?" she whispered, not wanting to use her voice at all. "Are you coming?"

"Hey! What are you doing down there?" A deep male voice boomed from behind, swinging her around by her upper arm. "How could you do this to me? After everything I've done for you. How could you go down there?" His eyes widened. "Unless… No. You wouldn't. Would you? Are you stealing from me, Rachelle?"

"No. No," Rachelle fumbled to pull words from her mind, which was still set to flight mode. The man's round face and balding wisps of hair registered in her brain as safe, except that the throbbing pulse at his temple didn't portray the message of safety. "Uncle Jerome. No, I'm not stealing anything. Someone shot at me down there."

"Shot at you? What are you doing down there? What are you talking about?" Her uncle raised his gaze over her head. "Who are you? Are you her accomplice?"

Rachelle craned her head around to find Gage on the bottom tread. She didn't know who looked madder. Her uncle? Or Gage?

"Take your hands off her." Gage's deep, lethal-sounding voice didn't leave any room for negotiating.

Uncle Jerome let go but didn't budge from his spot. "Who are you? Are you that diver she dragged in yesterday? If I find anything missing—"

"You won't, and I can't believe you would even think it." Gage climbed the rest of the way out and stepped up beside her. The message was clear where he stood, physically and symbolically.

Rachelle read the challenge in his eyes as a standoff ensued between him and her uncle. She placed her hand on his upper arm to get his attention. It was a nice sentiment but not needed. "Did you find anyone?" she asked Gage quietly.

"It's safe now," Gage announced with his gaze still locked on Jerome.

"What's safe? What are you talking about?" Jerome interrupted. "Someone else is down there? That's it. I'm calling the sheriff's office. You two get upstairs and find yourself a seat. You're not going anywhere until I know the tunnel's been cleared." He looked at Rachelle dead on. "And *nothing* better be missing."

Jerome nearly reached for her arm to cart her away like a common criminal, but one more deadly stare from Gage had her uncle rethinking the location of his hands. He dropped them to his side and gave a quick chin jut in the direction of the stairwell that led up to the dining room.

She grabbed the same table they sat in before. A silent conversation passed between them. It started with Gage's silent question expressed so well with his raised eyebrows. *Is Jerome always like this?*

Her nod said yes, but she couldn't elaborate that he had a valid reason. Soon all would be revealed, and Gage would understand. It wouldn't be long now before he knew what her father had done.

He let his eyes fall on the door with a nod that said it was okay to get up and walk out.

But that would only prolong the inevitable.

She shook her head.

He leaned back with a deep sigh and sent a pointed glance at his large, black diver's watch. Was he in a hurry? Jolene had said he only had twelve hours. To what, Rachelle wasn't sure.

Sheriff Matthews burst through the front door followed by his newest rookie deputy, Billy Baker.

Great. Gretchen's boyfriend. This couldn't get any worse.

Billy was the reason Gretchen had distanced herself from Rachelle after the arrest. He was going for the job and thought it wouldn't look good if his girlfriend hung out with a convict's daughter.

"What's going on, Jerome? What's this about someone shooting in your tunnel?" Sheriff Matthews asked his questions, but his eyes stayed locked on Gage. "And why am I not surprised to see you here, Fontaine?" He didn't wait for an answer but commanded them to stay put while he went with Jerome to check out the tunnel.

Billy strutted up to the table, appointing himself their guard. "Well, well, well. Looks to me like you're following in your father's criminal footsteps. Should we expect to find a dead body in the tunnel?"

"No." Rachelle lifted her chin at the deputy she could barely take seriously, having grown up with him her whole life on the island. She turned to Gage to tell him to ignore him, then remembered Gage's words about the shooter down in the tunnel. When Gage came back out, all he'd said was "It's safe now." What had he meant by that? How could it be safe with the pirates still out there? Unless… had he "taken care" of Jolene *permanently?* Would the sheriff find a dead body down there, after all? Was that why Gage was in a hurry to leave?

The idea that he might have killed someone made her want to weep. She didn't want to believe he was capable of such a thing. She wanted him to be different. Better than her father. Better than her.

"What were you two doing down there?" Deputy Baker lowered his voice as if to be conspiratorial. "Have you forgotten your father killed your uncle's wife in those tunnels? How could you do that to Jerome? How could you make him go traipsing back through them?"

Rachelle closed her eyes with the reminder of just how deep her tainting went.

And now Gage knew it, too.

With her chin tilted down, she peered out the tops of her eyes through her lashes to search Gage's face for his response. Earlier, at her mom's house, he'd said nothing could shock him, and judging by the blank face he wore now, he'd told the truth.

Or he held his repulsion in check well. She wished for a glimpse at his true feelings, so she would know how to react with him. Hang her head at his disapproval or lift her chin at his pity?

He kept her waiting, and she realized her lungs ached without breaths. Her chest seized with the pain of more than lack of oxygen, though. The impact of Gage's pending judgment felt like a kick to her heart. Somehow, his opinion felt different than the islanders'. Or maybe she just hoped it would be.

Then his answer came in the bright and genuine smile he wore so well. Instantly, his response felt more like an acquittal than a judgment, a release from all charges.

On a quick inhale, she felt her lips twitch, a smile of her own threatening to break through.

He knew her secret, and he didn't judge. She didn't have to worry about him holding her father's sins against her. She could relax and stop dreading what would happen when he found out.

The truth was out, and he didn't condemn or even pity her.

The feeling was freeing.

Rachelle relaxed back in her captain's chair with a sigh that turned into a full grin. A smile that trembled, then grew bigger as she looked at this man who had given her the gift of freedom.

"No one's down there now," Sheriff Matthews announced as he reentered the dining room in a rush. "But the door that separates Jerome's tunnel from mine is open. The lock was blown off. I need to go home to make sure the door to our house is still intact. Our entrance was bolted closed permanently last year after Miriam—"

"Miriam!" Rachelle jumped to her feet so fast Gage stood up out of concern. Something drained the blood from her face to the point he nearly reached for her across the table in case she fell. "We have to find her to make sure she's okay."

Sheriff Matthews held up his hand. "She's not at home. She's working at the school. Otherwise, you'd be looking at my back. It's okay, Rachelle, but I thank you for your concern. It shows me you understand the severity of what is going on around here." His expression turned threatening and moved onto Gage. "What *you* have brought to our island, Fontaine. I want you to know I've made contact with an old federal agent I used to work with. If you've got any skeletons hidden or warrants out there for your arrest, I'm going to know real soon."

Gage shook his head. "You won't find anything."

"Well, I wouldn't be doing my job if I didn't at least look."

Jerome came through the cellar door, pocketing his keys in his front jeans pocket. "All locked up and secure." He looked pointedly at Rachelle. "Please don't go in there again. The place should be refilled and sealed up forever."

Sheriff Matthews nodded in agreement and turned back to Rachelle. "Have you reconsidered staying with your uncle? I think it would be the safest place for you."

Rachelle shook her head. "I'll be fine."

"You can't stay at your place," Sheriff Matthews argued. "It's too secluded. It's not safe."

She crossed her arms. "I said I'll be—"

"She's staying at her mom's house," Gage cut in, and all eyes widened to match their hanging jaws. Before anyone could regain their faculties, he continued, "It's right here in the village on Main Street with neighbors and businesses close by. Plus, it's near the station. Easy to keep watch over. And I'll be bunking on the couch to stand guard."

Rachelle screeched. "What? No way! I am not staying

there. And I don't need any of you watching over me. I can take care of myself."

Sheriff Matthews headed to the door. "I don't like the idea any more than you do, Rachelle, but it'll have to do until I can get more enforcements on the island. Now, I need to get over to my house to make sure the basement door is secure. Baker, head down to the cove and make sure the other end of the tunnel is locked. Fontaine, I'll let you convince Rachelle that you standing guard at Violet's house is for the best, until I hear what my federal source has on you. Once again, don't leave the island." With that he fled the scene.

The other men quickly followed him out, leaving Gage to handle Rachelle. At least, she wasn't screeching anymore. Although, the heated glare spoke volumes.

"It's not for long, Rachelle. We're going to find Jolene—"

"We?"

He gave a quick nod. "We. The tunnels didn't work out as I'd hoped. I wouldn't want you in there even if there weren't any bad guys chasing you. But now, this means you go with me wherever I go and vice versa. Especially when you go out to sea to work. Got it?"

She bit her lower lip. "What about my mom? She's not going to like me being in her home any more than I want to be there."

"We'll figure it out."

"We?" she repeated his choice of word again. Her dark eyebrows arched high in doubt.

He smirked. "Yes, my little skeptic, we. Why does that surprise you?"

She shrugged. "This captain usually runs solo."

"Not anymore. You've got yourself a first mate. And our first destination is that cove Sheriff Matthews mentioned. Jolene had to have booked out of that tunnel real fast. There's no way she had time to cover her tracks. I'm fairly certain she must have left some clues of her whereabouts behind."

"Right!" Rachelle's eyes lit up at the idea, then grew suspicious. "But we'd better get there before Deputy Baker messes with the scene and covers up any evidence."

"That would be tampering, and illegal."

Rachelle shook her head. "For being so worldy, you really are naive. It's a good thing I'm the captain of this ship."

Gage bit back a smile and saluted her. "Then lead the way, Cap."

FIVE

To a ship passing by, the cove could go unnoticed. The way the cliff jutted out shielded its entry and isolated the sandy shoreline from view. Gage was pretty sure only the locals knew of its existence.

And those with a map.

Jolene had definitely been here. She was obviously using his maps to scope out the place to find the treasure. Gage was also certain his boat had been in here, too. Jolene probably hid it in here overnight, knowing the authorities would be looking for a ship out at sea.

And now, she'd pulled up anchor and disappeared with his *Getaway* again. His boat slipped through his fingers like the thick sand around his feet. Nothing left but assorted boxes from his cargo to say she'd been here at all.

Deputy Baker gave a few minutes of his time to search for clues but then got a call on his radio from the sheriff. Matthews sent a coded message that had the deputy jetting back to the station without a farewell.

Gage didn't care. He had more things to worry about than what a 10-44 on the radio meant. He kicked the sand from his feet, not caring where it flew.

"What's wrong?" Rachelle asked from where she stood, inspecting the boxes.

"My boat was here, and I lost her again. I've always been one step ahead of these people, and now they're one step ahead of me." He breathed the salty air deep into his lungs to try to calm down.

"I thought this was about justice. Not your boat." She stood, her arms on her hips. "Why does it sound like you care more about finding your boat than finding Jolene?"

"Because I have a job to do. People are depending on me to find the *Maria's Joy*."

"Oh, so this is about a treasure that doesn't exist. How about focusing on what is real, like the Uzi-carrying pirate in these waters."

"Jolene didn't leave any tracks behind. The sand is too thick for imprints. Baker already locked the tunnel entry up. There's nothing here to lead us anywhere."

"What about these boxes?" She waved at the heap at her feet. "They might have some kind of clue in them."

"These boxes are mine. She threw them overboard to make a point that she's one step ahead of me. Ha-ha, the joke's on me again."

Rachelle's shoulders slumped. She blew a strand of her sable-colored hair out of her eyes, then crouched down and pried the flapped lid open. "Books? These are filled with *books*?"

"I like to read. What's wrong with that?"

"But they're all the *same* book." She looked at him as if he'd grown three heads.

"They're Bibles."

"I know what they are. I can read."

He reached down and lifted one black leather-bound Bible with gold-leaf edging. "Well, then allow me to give you your very own letter from God. It was written with you in mind." He placed it in her hands because she was too dumbfounded to step away. No reason to waste the opportunity.

"Why do you have all these?" She still held it. He took that as a good sign.

"Just carrying on what Pete did. As he traveled the world, he brought the Good News to anyone who wanted it."

"I thought he was in the navy. He was a missionary, too?"

"No, but if he was going anyway, he would take them with him. There are a lot of people who have never seen one of these. People who go about their whole lives feeling lost and wondering what their purpose is. This book tells them they're being sought out." Gage couldn't help but smile, thinking about the thankful people at his last port. "You should see their faces when they realize they're not lost anymore."

Rachelle looked at the cover, then dropped it back into the box with a shake of her head. "You shouldn't give them false hope. Not everyone navigates around the world in a million-dollar yacht diving for lost jewels."

"It's not like I keep the jewels for myself, and at the moment, I'm yachtless."

"And it looks like it's killing you."

He shrugged. "You're right. I can't do my job without her. But it's more than that. She's the only home I have. That I've ever had." He picked up the Bible again and held it out to her. "There is hope, Rachelle. For everyone. Take it, and see for yourself."

She looked at it but didn't say no. Then she snatched it up and said, "Fine, but it's not like I have any time to read. I have a dangerous pirate to bring to justice, and that's the only thing I'm looking for right now." She headed back down the shoreline toward the town.

Gage watched her go with a smirk at her tough exterior. He turned back to lift a box up to take with him. When he stood and hefted the box onto his shoulder, the sun flashed in eyes. He blinked before he realized the cliff blocked the sun and couldn't have blinded him. So what did then?

His gaze shot to the top of the cliff and caught a shooter kneeling on the ledge and aiming straight for Rachelle.

"Rachelle!" he shouted, dropping his box to take off in a run. The sand wouldn't give him any traction and flew up all around him with each arduous step. She stopped and turned back, confusion swathing her face, until a rapid rat-a-tat sound echoed through the cove and the sand sprayed up around her feet. A quick dawning of fear settled on her face. He didn't have to tell her someone was shooting at her. She knew it.

She had nowhere to hide, and there was no way he could make it in time to cover her. She swung around to run, but flew back to the ground at an impact only a bullet could make before she could take one step.

"Rachelle!" Gage reached her in a rush. He dived to cover her even though he was too late. Nothing he did would change this course. Rachelle had taken a bullet because of him. She'd paid for his crimes.

"Please, God, please help me. Please don't let her die because of me. I didn't mean for this to happen. I didn't mean to make Rachelle pay for my sins." Gage spoke into Rachelle's hair with his cheek pressed up against hers.

"Ouch," she yelled out, and pushed at his heavy chest.

"Where are you hurt? Can you tell me?"

"My cheek. You haven't shaved in days."

He stilled and lifted his head to search her face. "Seriously? That's it?"

"Well, it hurts. Now get off." He didn't move except

to crank his head around to search the sky behind him. "She's gone. I don't see Jolene. It's probably safe to move." He turned back around. "Are you sure you weren't hit? I saw you fly back." He pulled up, keeping her out of view of the cliff as he patted down her arms and legs. "You are fine. I don't believe it."

Rachelle rolled to her side, not sure what had thrown her either. All she remembered was the sand spattering at her feet, and the next second a power as strong as the speed of light had sent her flying. It had to be a gunshot, but where?

Curling her toes and fingers as she gained her feet didn't reveal any injuries. Even the soft sand had offered a thick cushion in her fall.

She shrugged it off. "Whatever. It doesn't matter. I've escaped Jolene's attempt to take me down, and that's all I care about. Let's go. We have to find her before she succeeds."

Rachelle scoped out the cliff in all directions. She wanted to get moving but wasn't going to be a walking bull's-eye. At finding the cliff empty, she took quick steps to get out of the cove.

"Wait!" Gage yelled from behind. "I want you by my side from now on."

"Then you'd better keep up," she called back over her shoulder, and kept walking.

"Rachelle, stop!" From the distant sound of his voice, he hadn't taken one step to reach her. The man was letting that criminal get away!

She stopped all right. And swung to give him a piece of her mind. "Maybe you don't care to catch that woman because it wasn't you who she shot at, but if you want me by your side, then you'd better step lively. Because I'm not letting her get away this time. Now let's go."

He didn't move. A weird look settled on his face. Confusion, maybe? He stood there looking at her and not saying a word.

"What's wrong with you?" she called out.

His mouth moved silently a few times before he said, "I figured out where you were shot."

Rachelle tried to look behind her. He must have seen blood on her back. She didn't feel pain, but maybe she was in shock or something and couldn't feel pain, yet.

"Where?" she asked, stopping her search to look back at him.

He'd moved from his spot up to her side. In his hands was the Bible she'd been carrying before. She'd completely forgotten about it.

He lifted it up with the front cover facing her. A gaping hole exposed the backend of an exploded bullet fragment wedged inside the book. Gage reached a finger in to dig it out, holding the ballistic evidence in his palm. "I don't know about you, but I would call this hope." He handed it to her. "Jolene probably thought she hit her mark when you went flying back. What she didn't know was you carried the greatest shield of all time." He lifted the Bible.

Rachelle reached up to take the book in her other hand. With the bullet meant for her in one hand and the Bible in the other, her hands trembled to hold on to both. "This bullet could have hit me," she whispered in a stunned voice. She looked at the hole in the Bible. "And that hole could have been in me." She locked eyes with Gage. "I don't know what this means, *if* it means anything at all." She spoke louder when Gage opened his mouth to interrupt her. "*But* I will say, God obviously cares for you, so *if* He had anything to do with this, it was all for you, I'm sure. Now let's get out of here before Jolene realizes she missed me…and before I throw up."

* * *

"Good. You're here." Sheriff Matthews came out the front door of the Sheriff's station and met Gage and Rachelle on the crushed-seashell walkway out front.

"You already heard?" Rachelle asked, wondering why the lawman hadn't come to help if he knew Jolene had taken shots at her again.

"I didn't hear personally, but the rest of Main Street did. I was still at my house when the call came in. I sent Deputy Baker to the scene, but I got here as soon as I could."

"Here? What are you talking about? We needed you at the cove."

"Wait," Gage interrupted. "Does this have anything to do with that 10-44 code that came in on Baker's radio?"

Sheriff Matthews sealed his lips.

"Ten forty-four?" Rachelle searched their faces. "What does that mean?"

The sheriff hesitated with reluctance in his eyes before saying, "Suspected mental person causing a problem." He held up his hands. "But I didn't know who it was. All I had to go on was an islander's call, saying someone was yelling up and down the streets. I didn't know who it was until I got here."

"I don't understand, Owen." Rachelle waited for him to continue. "Who was it? And how does it have anything to do with me?"

Gage placed a hand on her forearm. She dropped her gaze to his gentle touch. Did he know who'd yelled in the streets? She raised her eyes to him to ask.

Gage looked to the sheriff. "It's her mom, isn't it?"

Sheriff Matthews pinched his lips. "I don't see how any of this is your concern, Fontaine."

"My mom? My mom was yelling? Wait." Rachelle felt her breath catch and her eyes widen. "My mom was out of the *house?*" The last part screeched from her lips and caused both Gage and Owen to shush her. "But Mom hasn't come out of the house in a year. What would make her come out now?"

Owen looked at Gage as if it was him, but that didn't make sense. "Gage was with me all day. It couldn't have been him. I wish you would stop treating him like the criminal and start looking for the real one. That woman shot at me *again* down in the cove. That's three times now. It also makes it three times she got away with it. While you're looking to pin something on Gage, I'm going to end up dead, and *she's* going to go free."

"I can assure you, Rachelle, I'm looking for her, too." He glanced quickly at Gage. "But don't let the pirate in the sailor suit fool you. I really would feel better if you distanced yourself from him."

"He's standing right here and can hear you."

"He's a big boy, and I really don't care if I damage his psyche."

"Right, because then you could send out another 10-44 code for another mental case, which by the way, I don't appreciate. My mom is not mentally ill and something other than her so-called psyche brought her out of that house. So, tell me who *really* got my mom to come out, because it wasn't Gage."

"It may not have been Gage directly, but he is the one that brought that woman here."

Rachelle felt the blood drain from her face. What was Owen saying? That Jolene went to go see her mom…and sent her screaming out of the house? Had she tried to kill her, too?

Rachelle ran at full speed through the station's front door. Both men tried to stop her, but she couldn't hear them over her own shouts for her mom. Rachelle ran from the empty main office to the empty back room, stopping at the locked door to where the two cells were located.

"You put my mother in a jail cell? Are you crazy? Don't you know what that will do to her?"

Owen stepped up with his hands raised. "Rachelle, Violet's not in there. I promise you."

"Then where is she?"

"I took her right to the clinic. She's resting right now. You can go see her. In fact, you really need to. She believes you're dead. That's what she was screaming about. She found a message meant for you."

Rachelle looked to Gage beside her, then back to Owen. "Wh-what kind of message?"

Owen shook his head. "It doesn't matter." He turned and headed back to the front office with her at his heels.

"Yes, it does, and you will tell me."

Owen stopped at his desk to open the lower drawer. He pulled out her camera and held it out to her. "I copied all the pictures of Jolene. Now take your camera and go see your mom, and stay low."

Rachelle held firm. "What was the message?"

Owen sighed and shook his head at Gage, who was standing in the doorway. "This is your fault. I am going to make you pay for this. I already heard back from my connection with the feds. They told me how the captain of your boat died suddenly two years ago. Even deemed it suspicious."

Gage's face paled a little. A slight blink to his eyes showed Owen's words had hit their mark. But when he spoke, he spoke with conviction. "Suspicious? He died of the bends."

"Says you. You can believe I'll be looking into it."

"You won't find anything, because I didn't do anything illegal. It may not have been right, but it wasn't illegal."

"We'll find out real soon. A federal agent will be here tomorrow. I'd say your days of freedom are numbered."

"You're right, they are, and I thank God every day for each one of them. Now show Rachelle the message so she can go see her mom."

Owen shook his head. "I don't think it's a good idea. Trust me, Rachelle. There's no reason to put yourself through the ordeal."

"Ordeal? What does it say?"

"It's not just a letter."

"What is it then?"

Owen bit his lower lip almost viciously but finally agreed with a single nod. "It's out back."

He led the way back through the office and then through the back room to the rear exit. Down the steps, Rachelle felt as if she were being led to her execution. No one spoke, the only sound between them the roar of the growing waves. The storm out at sea grew closer, but it was nothing compared to the one growing in her.

Owen stopped at some sort of box shape under a tarp. "Rachelle, I really want to ask you to reconsider this. There's no reason for you to see this."

"Stop babying me and lift the tarp."

Owen bent and, with a quick flick, revealed a lobster trap.

"My trap!" She stepped forward but halted when she saw something inside. "It can't be," she whispered even as she knew it was. "The hawk. Jolene killed the hawk?" Her voice caught as tears pooled up in her eyes.

Gage reached down to pull the tarp back over.

"Wait." She squeezed her eyes tight and knelt down beside the trap, reaching a finger in to touch the beautiful brown-and-red feathers. "I'm so sorry. I promise you I am going to get her and make her pay for this." She closed her eyes, letting the tears fall for a second—then she swiped them away with a vicious hand. She stood to her full height, which barely reached the men's shoulders, but no one needed height to take a stand. "This is a federal crime. Hawks are protected under the Migratory Birds Treaty Act. She has to pay for this. You said there's a federal agent coming. The agent has to know about this."

"And they will. You can count on it. But Rachelle—" Owen reached into his pocket "—I'm sorry to say, there was something else attached to the trap. This is what sent your mom screaming from her house. As if the bird wasn't enough."

Owen held out a note to her. Across the white paper, a short, but sobering message was scrawled with a heavy hand.

You're next, Lobster Lady. You're next.

SIX

"Whoa." Gage clicked through the digital pictures on Rachelle's camera. "I can see why Jolene wants you dead. Knowing you took these shots must infuriate her. She emerged from the water feeling pretty good about catching me off guard under the sea, only to have you catch her off guard above."

"Speaking of which—" Rachelle pulled open the glass door to the clinic "—if she wanted you dead, why did she stab you in the arm? Why not the heart?"

He followed her in, chuckling at the back of her swaying, silky hair. "Did anyone ever tell you that you're kind of vicious?"

She tossed her hair and looked at him. "Just answer the question." Her glittering green eyes flashed. How could he say no?

"She didn't want me dead. She just wanted to weaken me to get the upper hand and also to let me know she finally outsmarted me. Although, if I had happened not to make it back up alive, she wouldn't have cried. I was supposed to have raced to the surface, completely incapacitated with the bends. I would have had no choice but to become her prisoner and be taken back to Marcus. Her job done, except—"

"Except, I was in the wrong place at the wrong time and just happened to be passing by in the exact moment she jumped from the sea, with my lobster trap in hand."

Gage dropped his shoulders in remorse. "Yeah, apparently, in her victory of besting me, she planned to dine on your savory critters. I wish that was all she wanted to take."

"Take? As in her homicidal ambition to take my life? Is that what you mean?"

The lump of guilt lodged in Gage's throat multiplied in size and weight. It had been there since Rachelle had rescued him from the pirate's plan to take him captive, growing bigger with every attempt on her life because of him. Had he been saved only for Rachelle to take his place? He denied such an outcome and swallowed past the ache that wouldn't go away until he rectified the situation and made her safe.

"Yes, that take," he said. "I'll admit Jolene's ambition is stronger than I thought. Originally, I believed I could convince her to leave you alone by promising a cut in my profits, but I don't think any bartering with her will work." He held up the camera. "But, I also don't think you were in the wrong place at the wrong time. You were exactly where you were supposed to be. *I* was the one that brought the danger to you."

"Well, then make it up to me." She stood by the closed door to the room he had stayed in when he was brought here.

"Name it. Anything you want."

"Come in with me to speak to my mom." She brought her voice down to a whisper. "Because as much as I told Owen about her not being mentally ill, I'm really not sure at all."

"I see." He studied the hopelessness in her eyes and wondered what he could say to change them. "Rachelle,

I know I'm not a doctor, but I'm fairly certain depression is a disorder, not a disease. I'm sure that doesn't matter when it comes to the effects on the family. It's really hard to watch loved ones battle such sadness. It hurts everyone. I'm sorry you're both hurting now, and of course, I'll come in with you if that's what you want. This year sounds like it's been very tough to handle."

"All because of one person's choices."

Gage shook his head. "It doesn't have to be that way. Yes, our choices have a ripple effect on those around us, but we don't have to let it destroy us."

"How can it not?"

"Forgiveness. It's the greatest weapon. It's why God told us we must do it. Not a recommendation but a command. He knows that when we don't, that's when destruction follows. Destruction of our relationships. Destruction of our dreams." He paused and looked at the closed door in front of them. "Destruction of our minds."

"But what about justice? How does justice get served if we're forgiving everybody?"

Gage reached out and took Rachelle's hand. He rubbed his thumb across the toughened calluses that her hard work had put there. Toughened in the same way her heart had been. Some might see the calluses as evidence of being a victim, forced to labor as a result of another's poor choices. He flipped her hand over and gently rubbed across her fingertips. Some people would see them that way.

But not him.

Gage had come too far to go back to that way of thinking. "Jesus promises us two things," he told Rachelle. "Favor and vengeance."

She scoffed. He wasn't surprised. "I would be happy with just the vengeance," she spouted.

"I figured you would, but listen, your definition of

vengeance isn't God's. Vengeance isn't putting someone behind bars. It isn't kill before they kill you. It isn't retaliation. Vengeance is your testimony." He lifted her hand to show her the calluses. "It's the proof that you survived. That you made it. That you got back up. And because God is with you every step of the way, He helps you stand tall and above your circumstances, and when you get through it, *that* becomes your vengeance."

Rachelle withdrew her hand and looked at hardened bumps for long moments of silence. Finally, she looked up at him. "Will you tell my mom this? Because she hasn't gotten back up, and I really wish she would."

"Maybe we can show her how?"

"We?"

"Yes, we. Are you back to that again? I told you I'm not leaving your side."

"I know, but I—"

He reached for her hand and lifted it to her face. "Look. You got back up, Rachelle. You are the best person to tell her."

She sighed and blew out a few deeps breaths. He wished he could go in and make this all go away for her, but that wasn't his place. Still, he could stand beside her as she took hers.

"You ready?" he asked. At her nod, he said, "Then let's get your mom and take her home."

Rachelle opened the front door of her mom's house just enough to peer out at the relentless banging. "I thought you said it would only take you a couple hours to fix the porch."

Gage lifted his head from where he knelt on the lowest step. "Did I say that?" He flashed his cheerful smile in her direction. "I must have been being optimistic."

"Or bragging."

"That, too, but you can't blame a guy when he's in the company of a beautiful woman. He's going to say things to make her take notice."

Rachelle rolled her eyes. "The only thing I'm noticing is you're not done yet, and it's been two days, not two hours. I can't stay in here, Gage. I've cleaned every square inch of the place. I've got dust in my eyes, nose and mouth. I need to get out and get some fresh air. And I need to get back to work. My boat's ready. The windows are all fixed, and I've got full lobster traps waiting for me. The lobsters will start eating each other if I don't get them out."

"Sounds dangerous for you and gruesome for them, but honestly, your safety is my only concern. I don't think it's safe to be out on the water." The way he looked up and down the street slowly told her he was worried of what might happen if she stepped out of the house and into the sunlight.

She worried what would happen to her if she didn't.

Her mom sat behind her in the living room. She'd spent all day yesterday downstairs, and though Rachelle was happy to see her dressed and nibbling on the toast she'd made for her, Violet had still only said a few words to her.

The silence was brutal. The only thing worse was when Gage spoke to her mom, and she answered him with no hesitation. Rachelle had stopped asking why. She just needed to get out and feel productive. Productivity wasn't happening here, in her estimation, and she felt as useless as useless could be.

Gage gave two more pounds with his hammer and said, "All finished. It took longer because there was more rotten wood than I realized. I had to replace a lot of lumber to make it safe, but you ladies are styling now. This'll hold tight for you for years. And I'm not just boasting about my abilities. That's a fact. Long after I'm nothing more than a remembrance as the treasure hunter who visited Stepping Stones, you ladies will still be stepping out in safety."

"Visited?" Rachelle repeated the word that tripped her up. Visited meant one thing.

He was leaving.

Of course, he was leaving, she told herself. Stepping Stones wasn't his home. His home was at sea. Port to port. Treasure to treasure. The sea was in his blood, as he'd told her the first day they met. And the sea would be where he returned to.

Soon.

"Can we just go?" Her voice came out with a little too much gruff, but she cleared her throat and chalked it up to losing money. It couldn't actually be about Gage leaving. "My traps are going to be overflowing, and with each day I miss the market, my livelihood is going down the drain. Plus, if I don't return to my traps, poachers will set in and empty them for me."

"Are you sure your uncle can't grab them for you for the time being? I really don't think you should be out on the water. We haven't heard from Jolene for three days, but she's still around. I'm also pretty sure she's contacted Marcus by now. She gave me twelve hours to find her and board the yacht as her captive. I'm still here, which means she made the call. He could show up at any time. I want you nowhere near the sea when he does. I want you nowhere near me, for that matter."

"Are you saying he'll be taking shots at you like Jolene has been at me?"

"Don't be so happy about it."

"Just let me get my pots emptied. We'll come right back in. I'll go as fast as my boat can go. Promise."

Gage grumbled in indecision, but finally looped his hammer in his belt and stepped up to the door. "Fine, green eyes. We'll go." He leaned in so their faces were inches apart in the crack of the door. "But, the next time you ask me to do something for you, I would really appreciate it if you'd ask with your eyes closed."

"You call this fast?" Gage stood beside Rachelle in the wheelhouse of her lobster boat. He reached for the throttle, but it was already at full speed.

"I never said my boat went fast. I said I would go as fast my boat could go."

"And if *my* boat shows up in these waters, we'll never outrun her. Her engines are top of line." Gage grabbed her camera on the console and used the telephoto lens to study a spec of another boat off on the horizon. He visibly relaxed, so it obviously wasn't the *Getaway*.

He draped the camera strap around his neck and continued to look in all directions.

"Go easy with my camera," she asked. "It was a gift from my grandfather a few years ago. He's gone now, and I would be crushed if something happened to it."

"Understandable. That's how I feel about my boat. She's not just my home, but a gift." He flicked through her photos on the camera, bringing up one of the pictures she had taken the first day they met. "If I never see her again, can I get a copy of this one?" He tilted the camera toward her.

It was the picture she had taken at the back and side angle of the yacht. Jolene had already tucked herself away inside and was no longer on the deck. The name of the boat scrawled on the stern and a black flag with white lettering on it flew from the mast.

"What does your flag say?"

"It's Psalm 18:16. He reached down from Heaven and rescued me; He drew me out of deep waters."

"Aw, I see. The words you live by. That makes sense,

but the name of your boat doesn't. If you're not a criminal, why is she called the *Getaway?*"

"Pete named her after a hijack he intercepted before he retired. The mission was called Operation Getaway."

"Did it end positive?"

"For the navy, yes. For Marcus, no."

Rachelle took her eyes off the water to see Gage's face. "Are you serious? Isn't that rubbing it in and asking for trouble?"

"*Or* giving a message to any pirate who is even thinking about hijacking her. The navy always wins, so the pirates better think twice before they board with their guns." He lifted the camera and aimed it at her. Before she could object he hit the shutter release and captured her image.

"Hey! I don't like to be on this side of the camera."

He looked at the picture he'd taken and laughed. "And I shouldn't be on this side. You're a much better photographer than I am." He showed her a picture of herself taken much too close. "Don't delete it, though. I want a copy."

"For what?"

He shrugged. "Something to remember you by. When I'm sailing around the world on the long, lonely oceans, I'll have it to remember this day out here on the water with you."

Rachelle tried to smile through the sullen feeling his words brought on. Once again he'd made it clear he was moving on. He stated the obvious, but deep down inside, she didn't want to face it. For the first time in a year, life wasn't so lonely. Gage didn't look at her like an extension of her father or the daughter of the hermit woman.

All she could do was state *her* obvious. "I'm going to miss you when you go. Life on Stepping Stones will be unbearable again."

He brought the camera down to his chest to look at her

with no obstruction. "You don't need to keep your head in the sand, you know. It's okay to look people in the eye to make them realize you've done nothing wrong. If they can't look back, that's not a reflection of you. That's something they need to work on. You've risen above your circumstances with your will to survive and your hard work."

Rachelle brought the boat to a stop. "Speaking of hard work, get your gloves on. We're here. And did anyone ever tell you you're too optimistic?"

"Now, see, I thought I was keeping it real." He flashed the bright handsome smile she would miss so much. His reality made hers look drab and dank. She was certain he never wore bright-orange waders when he manned his boat. She pictured him at the wheel of his luxury yacht, the sun glinting off the clear water of the tropics, beautiful people lounging on his deck in bathing suits without a care in the world.

No, his reality wasn't hers, she summed up and got back to work. "Okay, your job is to cut bait, while I catch. You remember what I told you to do?"

Gage removed the camera and placed it back on the console. He grabbed a pair of bright blue rubber gloves that would protect his hands from the pinching claws of the lobsters. "I'm ready when you are. Let's do this quickly and get out of the water. The boat is slow, but sitting still out here is worse."

Rachelle grabbed the pole she used to lift the buoy out of the water. From there she worked on autopilot, attaching the rope to the pulley system and cranking up seven green metal traps. One by one, she opened the traps and scooped up the lobsters, tossing them into the blue barrels behind her or sending the young bugs back into the sea to live another day.

Gage restocked the traps with fresh bait, closed them up and pushed them aft along the railing where they waited all lined up neatly to be shoved back overboard.

"All seven traps emptied and restocked in half the time," she shouted to him with a fist pump from the wheel. "You can be my stern man any day!" Then she gave him the nod to push the first one back into the water while she piloted forward. Every thirty feet or so, he sent over the next one in line until they were returned to the bottom of the sea for the next catch.

As she unhooked the buoy from the pulley and tossed it back in, Gage came up behind her and shouted, "Nice work, Captain." He patted her twice on the back as she moved the boat forward. Once again she reverted to autopilot because all she could think about was the intense tingling his hand left behind on her back, even through the thick layers of rubber and cloth. "How many more stops do we have?" he asked.

"What?" she answered loudly, unable to formulate any other words, but he probably thought she hadn't heard him over the boat's chugging motor.

"How many more catches for today?"

She watched his moving lips and mouthed her own. "Three." After a few seconds, she looked up into his eyes as blue as the sky.

Except they darkened and looked away before she caught her fill.

Had she been too transparent about her growing feelings for him? The way he averted his gaze told her he didn't return the sentiment.

Rachelle pushed the throttle to move her boat onto another of her fishing locations. But what she really wanted was to fish for the answers on how Gage felt about her, if anything at all.

* * *

Three stops complete, one more to go before they could get out of these waters. Gage continued to inspect the sea around them, expecting at any moment to be ambushed again. If Jolene could catch him on the sea floor, then anything was possible. The idea of Rachelle being attacked out here dampened his spirits more than his wet jeans did. At least she stayed dry in her orange overalls…and looked adorable at the same time. She was so small and petite, her trousers practically swallowed her whole. But would they stop a bullet?

No.

Gage surveyed the area in a 360 degree turn. As far as his eyes could see, no boats approached, but he realized they were in the same vicinity of his last dive. He'd chosen this location as a potential site of the sunken *Maria's Joy.* His maps marked this area as the place to dive, which gave his heart a little jolt of excitement now…before he reigned it in.

What was wrong with him? Yes, the hunt was in his blood, but Rachelle came first. Period. But maybe later he could return…

"Hey, would you mind if I did a little treasure hunting with your boat? If I could find the treasure, it would sure give me the upper hand with Jolene and Marcus, when he arrives. I don't have my maps and documents, but I think enough of my prep work is tucked away in my memory. I could pull from that."

Her eyes lit up like the jewels he loved. "Will you let me join you? I've never hunted for treasure before. Just lobsters."

"No, *mi joya,* that's not a good idea. First, you'd have to be able to dive."

Her face fell. "That's a prerequisite?" She reached for

the buoy pole for the fourth time today. Gage resumed his place by the bait box to wait for her to lift the buoy out of the water. "I think I might prefer to stay above water," she said with her back to him. "But maybe I'd think differently if you taught me what I need to know."

The idea of strolling along the bottom of the sea with Rachelle made his heart rate speed up even more than hunting for the treasure had. He loved diving, loved being able to breathe underwater, but sharing the thrill with her would be so much more amazing. The idea of her being part of his life was…impossible.

He bypassed the obvious reasons of her safety under the present circumstances. That was a given. But even beyond the present circumstances, if either of them made it out alive, she could never be a part of his seafaring life. And he sure wasn't about to make terra firma his home.

As he'd originally thought, Rachelle being a part of his life was impossible.

He cleared his throat. "I don't think it would be a good idea for you to be out here. I don't like you out here as it is."

"I can handle myself, Gage, but fine, don't teach me. I understand what you're not saying." She turned away to lift the buoy and start pulling up the rope and traps attached. Her tug met with a resistance she didn't have the last three times. Gage figured she was getting tired until she said, "It must be caught on something." She leaned over the edge to pull with two hands. Just as he stepped up to help her get a hold of the rope, Rachelle flipped right over the railing with a quick yelp before she plunged down headfirst into the lapping water.

"Rachelle?" Gage paused at the edge, thinking she'd resurface right away. But after a few seconds of seeing no movement and hearing nothing but the motor and water splashing against the hull, he knew she wasn't resurfacing.

Were her overalls weighting her down? Had they filled with water? He didn't think so, but if they hadn't, then where was she? Why wasn't she swimming back up?

A sick feeling hit him dead center in the chest. If Jolene could catch him off guard below the water, then why couldn't she catch Rachelle, too?

Gage jumped up on the railing to dive into the water. He broke the lapping waves and immediately found the rope Rachelle had been after. His hands followed it down, hoping she was still attached, but when he came to a severed end, he realized someone had cut it from the traps below. But when? Before or after Rachelle fell in?

Or, had she been pulled in?

It didn't matter. The only thing that mattered was finding her before she became lost forever.

SEVEN

Rachelle's lungs burned without access to the air above the water's surface. She still wasn't sure what had happened. One second she was working above water pulling up the rope. The next she flipped overboard and sank straight down, headfirst, into the cold, dark ocean. Then, before she could turn back around and swim up, something yanked the rope she gripped in her hands. The force had pulled her sideways, and she flew through the water at least twenty feet before reason kicked in and she let go of the rope. Even though she hadn't been yanked downward, a wide gap above still separated her from breaking out of the ocean's hold.

Sunlight lit the surface and promised her life-giving air, but the distance to get there was unknown. She used every bit of strength she had in her to swim up. Her waders made it tough, and she quickly found the buttoned straps at her shoulders to unhook them. Her small frame swam right out of them, but when she looked up, the sunlight above dimmed. Rachelle squinted through the murky water and caught the end of a large fish tail wave as it went by above her. Its shape told her it wasn't just any fish.

It was a shark!

With no reserve air in her lungs, she pushed harder upward and hoped the shark didn't come back. She had to get back into her boat. Fast.

Her eyes took in the surface, looking for her boat's bottom. She found its dark hull about fifty feet away. It had to have been the shark that pulled her sideways. The fish must have grabbed her rope when she was pulling it out of the water and taken her for a ride.

But Rachelle needed to focus on getting out of the water, not how she'd been pulled in. The sunlight grew brighter. The surface grew nearer. Another few strokes and her face broke through, with inhalation after inhalation. Would her lungs ever be full again? She struggled to stay afloat.

Water lapped at her face, and the stem of her boat had never looked so daunting as it hovered over her. How would she get back in from the bow? She'd have to swim around to the stern. But what if the shark came back?

Now that she had air in her lungs, the severity of her situation squeezed her chest in electrifying panic. At any second, she could die. In any moment, a set of teeth could sink into her.

Suddenly, her new air supply began to disperse. In her state of fear, her breaths sped up to a choppiness that matched the waves. *Stay calm. Stay calm,* she said with each stroke closer to the boat.

"Rachelle!" Gage's voice shouted out around her. Was he in the boat? He had to stay there.

"Stay...stay in the...the boat!" Her words barely made a sound against the motor of her boat and the waves around her. "Shark!"

In the next second, something hit Rachelle in the back. She screamed, and her arms and legs flailed in all directions. She tried to remember how to stun a shark. Did she need to hit them on the side of the nose, or the front? And how would she know where she was hitting anyway?

Her arms reached for her boat like a scared child for her mother.

Before she could kick out again, her head was yanked back and something came around her neck. Her hands went to her throat to feel an arm. It pressed in, cutting off her cries. "I've got you, Rachelle. Stay calm so I can get you to the boat without you drowning both of us."

"Gage!" His name burst from her lips. She realized her whole body shuddered in his grip. Shock? Was she going into shock? "Shark…" He had to know before she did. "Shark in the water."

"Sharks are nothing to fear." He sounded so calm. How could he be so calm? Did he not hear her? Did he not understand?

"Shark! Shark!"

"Shh." His cheek touched hers. She didn't care about his stubble now. The abrasion told her he was with her and she was alive. For now. "We're almost there. You're going to be fine. Trust me. I've encountered a lot of shark species on my dives. You're not on their dinner menu."

She opened her eyes, not even sure when she'd closed them. Her boat was no longer in front of her. Panic reared up again as she tried to twist her head back and forth to find it. But the grip Gage had around her neck wouldn't let her move even one inch. He had her in a rescue hold.

"We're here." Gage spoke behind her. That's when she realized he must have turned her around to bring her back to the boat. "Do you have enough strength to hold on to the railing until I can get in to pull you up?"

"Yes." She thought she did anyway, but when he placed her hands on the railing so he could climb aboard, her arms felt as flimsy as string cheese and her fingers slipped down, losing their grip. Gage grabbed hold of her wrists to swoop her up in one lift just in time.

He laid her down on the deck, cradling her head on his arm. He pressed his face down into the crook of her neck, saying nothing. Only his heavy breathing could be heard in her ear. His chest rose and fell at an alarming speed, giving credence to the panic he, too, had been in even though he'd seemed so calm in the water.

"I—" Rachelle started and stopped, trying to catch her breath as her adrenaline plummeted. "I don't want to dive."

Gage shook his head and lifted it to look her in the eyes. He shook it again. "You don't have to."

"You can still use my boat to find your treasure. Just don't make me go down with you."

"Deal." He smiled, but it didn't bring his face to life like it usually did. No laugh lines this time. This time it was a smile that bordered tears. "I was so scared when you didn't come back up. I didn't know how I was ever going to find you. I was so sure it was Jolene who had pulled you in."

Rachelle had to laugh. It was either that or cry a puddle of tears to match the puddle of seawater seeping from her clothes around her. "Jolene? I'm not sure what could be worse? A shark or Jolene?"

"Jolene, by far. Sharks have a bad rep, but the truth is you have a greater chance of a vending machine falling on you than you do a shark attack. If you were bleeding, I would be concerned for your life. The creature could attack if it smelled blood. Thankfully you weren't. And thank God it wasn't Jolene down there this time." He leaned back to release her, but her hands reached for his. "It's all right. I'm just going to the wheel to get us home."

"Home? You called Stepping Stones home."

"I meant your home. That's all. Just rest and hang on. I'll get you there safely in a little while."

With that he made his way to the helm and kicked in the engine that had continued to idle the whole time. Sadness overcame her and tears spilled from the edges of her eyes. She knew physiologically they came from the drop in her adrenaline and the shock of her misadventure wearing off, but she had to wonder if they also leaked from her eyes because Gage would never see Stepping Stones as his home.

And after her deep-sea swim she could never see a life at sea as hers.

EIGHT

"Are you sure you don't want me to carry you the rest of the way? It won't be any trouble." Gage held tightly on to Rachelle's arm while she leaned her petite frame into him, wobbling with each step.

"I'm fine. I don't need any more strange looks from the islanders, and you carrying me through town would surely get the tongues wagging over at the Underground Küchen."

"The Underground what?"

"It's German for kitchen. There's a German restaurant on the opposite end of the boardwalk from the Blue Lobster."

"The competition?"

"Sort of, but really only in jest. Two of the men who made Stepping Stones their homes back after World War II started the restaurants. One was German, one was French, but they were the best of friends. My grandfather was the French one. Since his death, Uncle Jerome runs the restaurant now, but he's made it pretty clear he would rather eat what Tildy is cooking."

"Tildy?"

"She's the owner of the other restaurant now. And the first one who would be wagging her tongue if she saw you carrying me."

Gage itched to lift Rachelle up in his arms and let them all talk. But then he thought about the aftermath when he left the island, and how she would have to face the people alone. He didn't need to add more juice to the fire. But even so, he wouldn't be letting go of her arm completely. If people talked because of that, then he would say, let them. "So, Tildy took over for the German man. Has he passed on, too?" he asked as they reached the porch of her mom's house.

"Nope, Len Smith is still alive," she said as she walked up his new stairs. It had been a long time since he built stairs from scratch. The last set were from an odd job he'd taken as a teen, only to have the twenty bucks he earned confiscated by his latest foster father.

Rachelle turned with a soft smile that pulled him from his past reflections. He'd much rather focus on her any day. He smiled at her and liked having her at his eye level with her a step up from him. He noticed a light dusting of freckles on the bridge of her nose. If nothing else, the sun today had been good for her. "Len is a grandfather to us all," she said almost reverently. "He's over ninety years old and the last of the three patriarchs of the island."

"Three? Who was the third?"

"He's passed. You haven't met Miriam yet. She's Sheriff Matthews's wife. Hans was her grandfather, and he died quite a few years ago. It'll be sad to see what happens to Stepping Stones when Len passes. He'll be missed by everyone. I hope the island doesn't change for the worse."

Gage watched the green of her eyes mist up like an early-morning fog over a grass field. "You love Stepping Stones." At her silent nod, he understood her pain clearly. "You've dedicated your life to the island's prosperity." He reached out and touched the camera that hung from her neck. "You've captured the essence of its vitality in your photos. You've earned your place here, not because you were born here, but because you do everything you can to see it thrive and continue on. But yet, you do it all from afar."

Her emerald eyes flashed. His words broached dangerous shores. The pirates of the eighteenth century would have backed up from Stepping Stones and sailed right on at such a daring look.

But Gage took the dare. "Life isn't always supposed to be experienced behind a telephoto lens. Sometimes you have to get up close and personal to fix something."

She reached for the handholds on her camera. "And you know this because of all the people you hang around with at sea? If someone's living afar, it would be you."

"My home is the sea. I thought you also shared that love, but after today, I can see you don't. Yours is this island and its people. The people you wish would see how devoted you are to them and their home. And I'm sure they would be able to if you got close enough."

"Your rose-colored glasses are starting to make me ill. Here's your reality check, Gage. They don't want me getting too close. They think I might be just like my father, and they're right. I might be."

The front door opened, catching them both by surprise. Especially when it wasn't Violet standing at the door but Sheriff Matthews.

"I need you both to step inside," he said, using his body to prop the screen door wide for them to pass.

Gage locked gazes with the officer as he crossed the threshold, but Owen's blank expression didn't allow for a reading on what awaited them inside. "What's going on, Sheriff?"

No answer, but the huge man dressed in tan and wearing an NCIS cap said it all.

"I see the agent finally showed," Gage observed before introductions were made. No sense in letting them set the stage. "I thought he was due here yesterday."

The man stepped up but didn't offer his hand, not that Gage expected him to. After all, he was here to investigate him. "Gage Fontaine. I'm Special Agent Caden, Naval Criminal Investigative Service. We finally meet. I've been hunting you down for years."

"I can't imagine why you'd be looking for me, but I do tend to stay under the radar. I don't usually like company along for the ride."

"Is that why Pete Masters had to die?"

Gage jolted. He knew it showed, too. "Pete died of decompression sickness because of a low tank. I didn't mean for him to die." He looked to Owen but saw Violet behind him, quietly watching from the stairs. She looked petrified, and he couldn't blame her. He wasn't getting the warm and fuzzies, either. "What's this all about? Pete died two years ago. The authorities didn't question anything as suspicious."

"That's because they didn't know they were dealing with the death of a retired intelligence specialist. One of Pete's family members thought NCIS should know about the death. I worked under Pete and knew he didn't make mistakes that would cost him his life, so I took the case. I ordered a full military autopsy and learned ether was found in his blood."

"Ether? He died of the bends. That's when your body creates nitrogen to try and compensate for the change in elevation. The tank was low on oxygen. I thought I filled it. Pete got to the bottom of the ocean and ran out. He had to resurface too fast, causing his blood to bubble up with nitrogen. That's what killed him."

"As you're aware the tank was taken by the police."

"So?"

"So, NCIS also got a look at it. The tank wasn't empty, but it had been tampered with. Someone put ether in it."

Special Agent Caden and Sheriff Matthews both moved in beside Gage. The temperature in the room felt like it spiked. Why did it feel like an ambush was about to ensue?

Caden leaned in. The guy took up a lot of space, but for the agent's large size, his eyes were small though not weak. The lethal look emanating from the golden irises demanded a confession.

Gage refused to give any more space up to him. "There's no way you have anything on me, because I've done nothing wrong."

"Except someone had to tamper with that tank. Someone had to put ether in it. And a lot of it. More than any human can take in and still survive. As you said, you were the one to fill it. Are you positive you filled it correctly?"

Gage's blood pumped loudly through his head. Agent Caden's words sounded muffled, but his point came across crystal clear.

Someone had killed Pete, and Agent Caden believed it was him.

"What's going on here?" Rachelle involved herself in the conversation. "Owen, I thought the federal agent was brought here to catch Jolene. They have to arrest her. She killed the hawk, and she tried to kill me. Did you forget that?"

"Rachelle," Gage spoke before Owen could, but he kept his eyes on Caden, "take your mom and go upstairs. Get some dry clothes on before you get sick. Everything's all right here. They're just asking me some questions. And, if what they're saying is true, I'd like to get to the bottom of this, too. Pete was my best friend. He was more than a friend. He was my only family. If someone killed him, I'm going to want to talk to whoever did it. Go ahead. Take Violet upstairs. Please."

Her huff indicated she wasn't too happy with any of them right now, but she did as he asked. Out of the corner of his eye, he watched Violet clinging onto her daughter as they stepped up the stairs. Rachelle could really start to stand stronger if she had her mother back in her life. Both of them needed to take their rightful places in the community. Maybe a visit to Tildy's place could help. He'd think more on that later. For now, he needed to speak frankly with the federal agent. The man was here to investigate him. But maybe Gage could turn this to his own benefit. Maybe his running days could be over. He'd thought long and hard since Rachelle asked him if he was tired of running. The answer was yes, but if he wanted to be free from his past, then he would need to come clean.

Gage listened for the bedroom door upstairs to latch closed. When silence followed, he nodded to a chair behind Caden. The agent moved to his left and Gage stepped into the living room and took the seat. The other two men looked at each other, briefly before finding seats as well.

"Are we going to get a confession, Fontaine? Just like that?" Agent Caden took out a recorder. Gage opened his mouth to tell him to put it away, but the beautiful word *freedom* echoed in his head and stopped him.

"You're going to get my honesty. In return, I'd like your help in ending a chase that began fifteen years ago. I promise you, if you do, you'll have your killer. Because there's only one man who would want Pete Masters dead. And it's the same man who wants me dead."

Rachelle rubbed the sleep from her eyes and stepped off the bottom tread of the stairs to find an empty living room. After Gage sent her upstairs earlier, she'd changed and fallen fast asleep, but the need to find out what the federal agent planned to do about Jolene woke her up with a start. She didn't think she'd been out for that long, but the officers were gone.

"Gage?" she called, and went to the kitchen to find that room also empty. Her steps picked up through the rest of the house. She peered out through the windows to the shoreline out back only to come up empty there, too.

Gage was gone.

Had Owen taken him into custody? The idea made the storm inside her swirl up. It wasn't fair. Only criminals belonged behind bars. Gage wasn't a criminal. He was... he was...

What was he? And what was he to her?

A friend. That's what. Even if he set sail tomorrow and she never saw him again, he would always be a friend. She couldn't let him spend even one night in the jail cell. She would do what she had to do to bail him out.

The camera around her neck became her focus. Her only possession worth anything. But she would sell it for her friend.

Rachelle opened the front door with a purpose in mind. Her steps quickened down the new front stairs her friend had fixed for her mom. Not for any reason but to selflessly help. He was a good man, and the law needed to know this.

She made her way to the street and locked her eyes on the Sheriff's station three blocks down. The streetlights were on. That meant it was after six. The sun would set soon, but it wouldn't take long to get there and get back before the sky turned completely dark.

Hopefully, Gage would be with her when she returned and she would have her bodyguard back. She bit back a smile as she set out in a direct line for the station.

Okay, so maybe he was more than a friend, she admitted. At least to her. But, so what? It was just a little crush. And who could blame her? The man was beautiful in a rugged, windswept sort of way. She could so picture him at the helm of his boat, a look of contentment on his handsome face at being where he belonged. She could almost imagine his bright blues glowing with excitement at finding his next treasure. He thrived on it. She just knew this about him. It was what gave him purpose.

She wondered what gave *her* purpose and looked down at her camera. Could she really give it up? For Gage to be treated fairly and not put behind bars unjustly, yes.

She walked on.

At one block left, the front door to the station opened, and out stepped Deputy Baker and…Gretchen.

Rachelle halted, her sneakers skidding to a stop. Paralyzed for a moment, she stood there, thoughts of jumping into a bush came to mind. Yet, her feet stayed locked in place.

Her fingers dug into the palms of her hands as she faced the decision to fish or cut bait. Her calluses ran roughly against her skin, bringing to mind Gage's words. *You survived…you made it…you got back up. And because God is with you every step of the way, He helps you stand tall and above your circumstances, and when you get through it, that becomes your vengeance.*

Rachelle was pretty sure God wasn't with her every step of the way, but Gage was right about the surviving part. For that reason alone, she would face Gretchen head-on.

Gretchen turned at the sidewalk and noticed Rachelle for the first time. Her feet stopped just as Rachelle's had. Her pale complexion turned a shade lighter. Would she be the one to flee? And what if she did? Did that make Rachelle the winner? Would vengeance be served?

Rachelle didn't think so. She thought if her old friend

turned away now, all she would feel is sad. Then and there, she made the decision to reach out first.

"Hey, Gretchen."

Gretchen's mouth slackened, but she said, "Hey. How are you?"

"I'm fine. Well, not fine, really. Things are really crazy scary right—"

"Gretchen, we have to get going if we plan to keep our table," Deputy Baker interrupted. Not that Rachelle was surprised. After all, it was he who requested Gretchen keep her distance from the town pariah, so he could be the next deputy.

But it was Gretchen who agreed. She could have told him no. The fact she hadn't still hurt. Rachelle was about to say forget it, but Gretchen spoke first.

"We're not going to lose our table. My mom owns the place. Give me a minute. I want to talk to Rachelle for a little while. Why don't I meet you there?"

"It's not safe for you to be with her."

Rachelle frowned. "I hate to admit it, but he's right. It is dangerous to be around me right now. Don't worry about it. You go on. Maybe we'll catch up some other time." *Like when the gestapo isn't breathing down our necks.*

"No, now." Gretchen closed the gap between them, leaving her boyfriend behind.

Rachelle felt as shocked as Billy Baker looked. His stunned eyes locked on her, but quickly turned cold. A chill shook her, but in the next second Gretchen's warm arms wrapped around her and all thoughts of Billy Baker melted away.

"I want you to be careful," Gretchen whispered into her ear. "Everyone's talking about you. We're so worried. We want you to be safe. I don't want anything to happen to you. Do you hear me?"

Rachelle nodded because she couldn't believe it was Gretchen saying these things. Gretchen who turned her back on her during the darkest time of her life. *Hadn't she?* Or had Rachelle had a part in the fallout, too? Friendships *were* hard to sustain when one person went into hiding. "I will. I promise. I'm not going to let this woman win."

Gretchen pulled away to face Rachelle. "I heard she's a pirate. Steals ships and stuff. How did you end up in the middle of something like this?"

Rachelle shrugged and said, "Well, there I was, just minding my own business when out popped a diver poaching on my line. You know me, I couldn't let her get away with that."

"You should have. Maybe she would have just disappeared."

"Not without Gage, she wouldn't have."

"Gage? That's the man I've heard about. I heard he's a pirate, too."

"No, he's so good. He's helped my mom so much. She talks to him when she won't even talk to me. And he's protected me. Stayed by my side every step of the way."

Gretchen looked down the street toward Violet's house. "Well, then, where is he now? Why are you out here by yourself?"

"He would have been with me if Owen didn't have his contact from the feds show up and arrest him. That's why I'm heading to the station. To see about bailing him out."

"What are you talking about? Your pirate's not there." Gretchen turned around and called out, "Billy, the guy hasn't been arrested, has he?"

"Not yet, but we're working on it. You almost done chatting? We gotta go."

She looked back at Rachelle. "See? He's not there."

"Where is he then?" Rachelle mumbled aloud.

"Beats me, but something tells me you shouldn't trust him, either. I meant it when I said I want you to be careful. Come on, I'll walk you back to your mom's." She pulled Rachelle's arm to start walking. "Billy, we're taking her back to the house first."

Rachelle was grateful Gretchen took over, because at the moment she was too stunned to make a move. Where was Gage if he hadn't been arrested? Why did he leave her side? He'd promised to protect her.

At the front door she disengaged from her old friend. How many nights had Gretchen spent here growing up? The two of them had been inseparable, and now they felt like strangers. But yesterday they were enemies, so the upgrade to strangers was a good thing. "Thank you, Gretchen, for walking me back."

"I couldn't leave you out there. But I might not be around the next time. Stay inside and be safe."

Rachelle nodded and glanced beyond Gretchen's caring expression. Billy caught her attention with his incensed eyes still locked on her. He leaned against the lantern pole in the street, arms crossed. "Your boyfriend's not happy you're talking to me."

"It's just because he loves me and doesn't want me to get hurt."

Rachelle did her best not to roll her eyes. Instead, she forced a smile and said, "Good night."

Once the front door was closed behind her, and Gretchen couldn't see, Rachelle leaned against the door and gave in to the eye roll.

But then, who was *she* to throw stones? Gage had run out on her without even a goodbye. She crossed her arms but kept her own fuming under control. However, when and *if* Gage showed his face again, she might not be able to keep it under wraps.

A scream from upstairs echoed through the house, followed by a loud crashing sound that resembled glass breaking.

"Mom? Is that you?" Rachelle called, moving slowly toward the first step. The sound of a fist making contact against flesh jolted Rachelle into motion. Her mother had been upstairs alone, but not anymore. Rachelle had nothing and no knowledge to fight an intruder. She needed help.

The phone on the table by the stairs pulled her forward. She dialed 911 and let it ring three times, but the sound of someone hitting the wall had her dropping the receiver for the vase next to it.

"Go away, Rachelle! Now!" her mother yelled back. Her next word was muffled. Muffled but still clear. "Run!"

The Underground Küchen bustled with life and fellowship. One step into the warm, welcoming environment told Gage this was the community Rachelle loved. These were the people she used to sit with at her restaurant and chat with. Did they know how much she missed them?

Did they miss her?

How could they not? She was sweet. Honest and kind. Strong and beautiful. A smile he couldn't hold back broke his lips so wide his cheeks hurt.

"Ah, someone's in love. I'd recognize that smile anywhere," a male voice from the bar spoke over the boisterous conversations. Had the person been referring to Gage? He wasn't in love. That wasn't even a possibility. But whoever spoke quieted down the camaraderie in the room and now all eyes were on Gage, waiting for his answer.

"Who me?" He pointed to himself, searching the bar area for the man who had put the attention on him. "Do you always put your guests on the spot as soon as they walk in?"

Heads bobbed below a huge painting of a German countryside. The picture, along with the patron's expectant faces, invited him to feel at home.

And be honest with his answer.

"Okay, maybe just a little." He pinched his thumb and forefinger. "But she's adorable, and I'm sure every person here is half in love with her, too. Maybe you've heard of her. Her name's Rachelle Thibodaux."

All smiles vanished. Even the ones in the back corner sitting by the unlit brick hearth. But even though the smiles all disappeared, it wasn't animosity that replaced them on the faces staring at him.

It was sadness.

"How is Rachelle?" The voice that started this whole conversation asked from the bar, and now Gage could see it was an ancient-looking man. This had to be Len Smith, the grandfather and last remaining patriarch of the island. And the man Rachelle loved like family. Judging by the concern on the old man's face, and everyone else's in the room, for that matter, they thought the same of her.

"She's in danger." Gage kept his head high as he admitted, "And I brought it to her."

"We heard. The question we have for you is what are you planning to do to get her out of it?"

"That's why I'm here. Rachelle probably wouldn't be very happy with me right now if she knew I was here doing this, but I need to ask you for your help."

"Us?" the old man cackled. "How are we supposed to help you?"

"You could start by telling me anything you know about the pirates that used to live here. If I could find their sunken ship and the treasure she took down with her, I might be able to bribe the pirate queen to sail away peacefully."

The old man scratched his thin hair resting on the top of his head. "Son, if we knew where a ship sunk its treasure don't you think we would have found it ourselves a long time ago?"

"True enough, but maybe you have some clues. Maybe the pirates left something behind, but you didn't know what to make of it. I could take what you have and compare it to my notes and research. It just might lead me to the *Maria's Joy*."

"Then what? You take it and disappear? Leaving Rachelle to deal with this woman trying to kill her alone? Why should we trust you?"

All heads swiveled back to Gage for an explanation, and judging by the raised eyebrows and skepticism in their eyes, he knew it had better be a good one. But what could he say about himself? He was a man without a home. A man without roots. Nothing to say he was a man of good standing anywhere.

But maybe this wasn't about him.

"Because..." Gage stopped but knew what he wanted to say even if it wasn't what they were looking for. "Because Rachelle needs peace. More than anything else, she needs peace."

"Ain't that the truth," a woman behind the bar chimed in. Her blond hair was teased up in some fifties retro-looking poof. Her white apron stood out starkly against her blue German dress. She reached over and opened a drawer, bringing out a flashlight. Passing it over to Len, she said, "I say help him. He's got Rachelle's best interest at heart."

Len pushed his crooked body off the bar stool. "You heard the lady, son. If Tildy says to help you, then that is what we all will do. Follow me."

Gage looked at the patrons, then at the woman. He

mouthed *thank you* and picked up his step to reach the old man as he pushed through the kitchen's swinging doors.

"Where are we going?" Gage asked as they passed a chef and waitress. Len held open a door to a stairwell.

"Into the caves. You asked if there was something left over by the pirates. I've never understood it, but as you said, you might be able to make sense of it."

"This restaurant is connected to the caves, too? My last time in them didn't end so well."

"Not to worry. It's not connected to the other tunnels. It just leads up to my house. I use this stairwell multiple times a day. And so does everyone else."

"Everyone? Has Rachelle been here? She said she hates the tunnels. They give her the creeps."

"They give us all the creeps, but as you can see mine are lit up nice and have a solid set of stairs. Rachelle's run up and down these stairs her whole life. Her grandfather was one of my best friends. I miss him greatly."

"He died recently, correct? Rachelle's mentioned him."

"About a year now, and I feel like his death aged me. I'm definitely not as spry as I was a year ago."

"It's amazing that you walk up and down these stairs multiple times a day."

Len laughed. "Tildy keeps saying she wants to install an electric chair, and I guess I should let her."

The stairs ended and the ground evened out before another small set of stairs led up to a doorway, presumably Len's house.

"Are we going into your home?"

"Nope, you're going in there." He pointed a gnarled finger behind Gage's right shoulder. Gage turned and looked for a door, but there wasn't one. Then he saw a shadow of an opening. A thin crevice in the stone wall. "It's not lit,"

Len said as he clicked on the flashlight and passed it over. "It's a small opening, so you go on in alone. I'll wait here."

"What am I looking for?"

"You'll see it. Trust me."

Trust him? The man was old and hunched over. Gage figured he wouldn't jump him when he turned his back. And if he did, Gage would probably applaud his heartiness.

Gage stepped up and turned sideways to fit into the crevice. A small room opened up, but no one would be dancing in here. If he took two steps in any direction, he would hit a wall. Turning around, he flashed the light in all directions. As far as he could see nothing was in here.

Then the light shone on a word.

Gage paused and stepped back to grow the light on a wider surface. More words carved in the stone lit up.

Gage's heart rate picked up. Excitement stirred. Were the words a clue to the location of the *Maria's Joy?* He lifted the light to the top to find the first line and read aloud:

"There are three things which are too wonderful for
me, yea, four which I know not;
The way of an eagle in the air;
the way of a serpent upon a rock;
the way of a ship in the midst of the sea;
and the way of a man with a maid."

Gage read it three times, then mumbled, "That makes two of us who don't understand." He chewed his lower lip, racking his brain for any memory of his notes that might tie in with what this was. "This is from the Book of Proverbs, right?" He called out to Len.

"Proverbs 30:18-19 to be exact. Don't ask me why it's here, because I have no idea. I'm not even certain it was written by the pirates. I can't imagine there were many God-fearing pirates." The old man cackled. "All I know is it was here long before my friends and I arrived to settle on the island. I was hoping it would ring some bells with you, but you don't sound too excited. It must not match up to any of your research, I take it."

Gage shook his head. "I wish I had my notes to go through, but off the top of my head I'd have to say no."

"Well, fiddlesticks. That's all I've got for you. I guess we're not going to be much help for Rachelle, after all."

Gage exited through the crevice and shut off the flashlight. He handed it back to Len and followed the man back down the stairs in disappointing silence. He needed his boat and maps. That would be the only way to find the treasure. Maybe he should let Jolene know he'd do whatever she wanted. Help her find the *Maria's Joy,* and then what? Let her take him back to Marcus to be killed?

And what about Rachelle? How would his death help her? If he thought for a second Jolene would sail away and leave Rachelle untouched, he would go with the pirate in a heartbeat.

Maybe I should leave anyway. It would be best for Rachelle. His presence in her life had brought her nothing but pain when her heart already ached because of her disconnect from the islanders. If only he could help her reconnect with them.

Facing Len's back, he felt an idea sprout up. Len led the way back into the friendly dining room. Gage could picture Rachelle smiling and laughing with them all. As it should be. "You know, Len, maybe you can still help Rachelle."

Len turned around. "Name it."

Gage liked this man and his quick willingness. "If I could get Rachelle to come here, could you organize a little get-together, or something?"

"My birthday is coming up on Saturday. There's a party already being planned. Would that work?"

"That would be perfect."

"I'll make sure the whole island is here, but I have to say, I've got the easy part. You've got your work cut out for you, son. Getting Rachelle here is going to be near impossible. She would rather die than face any of us."

The image Len's words brought on did not sit well with Gage. "I'll make sure it doesn't come to that."

"Well, look who's here?" Deputy Baker entered through the front door with a young blonde woman trailing behind him. He headed straight for Gage and met him eye to eye. "Len, you actually let this pirate in here. You've been warned not to trust him."

"Billy, I'll make my own mind up on who I trust and let in here. You might want to remember that yourself."

The young rookie's jaw ticked, but he held back. "Always a joker, Len. I get it. This is your place. You're in charge. I'll respect that. But out there…" Billy jerked his head in the direction of the front door and the town beyond it. "Out there is mine. And speaking of keeping the peace—" he directed his attention onto Gage "—I just came from meeting up with Rachelle in front of the station."

Every part of Gage's existence turned to full alert. "What was Rachelle doing out of the house? I just left her a little while ago. She was sound asleep."

"She was looking for you," the blonde girl chimed in. "But don't worry, we saw her back to her house."

"Gretchen, stay out of police business," Billy shot over his shoulder.

"She was my friend, and I want her to be safe," the young woman replied with a little impatient edge to her voice. She looked to be about the same age as Rachelle. They probably had been friends, like she said. So what happened? Gage wondered. Had their friendship been that fragile that it could crumble under the sins of Rachelle's father? "Sir," she said, looking back at Gage. "She thought you'd been arrested, but she was ready to fight for you. I hope you're worth her allegiance."

Gage nodded, but the young woman, Gretchen, didn't look convinced.

The radio at Deputy Baker's belt chirped. "Ten thirty-one at twelve Main. Need backup."

Gage's full-alert status returned. "That was Owen. And that's Violet's house."

Baker bolted from the restaurant, Gage right on his heels.

"What's a 10-31?" Gage shouted as they ran down the boardwalk and up to Main Street. At Baker's nonresponse, he asked again with more bite to his words.

"It's a crime in progress!" the young man shouted back.

Crime in progress. A crime going on right at this very moment.

A crime going on right now against Rachelle.

NINE

Taking the stairs two at a time, Rachelle reached her mother's room with vase in hand. Twisting the knob and throwing the door wide, she ran in before she could think twice and hoped the element of surprise would be on her side.

Except that Jolene stood by an open window with one arm wrapped around her mother's neck and a gun to her head.

The pirate had been expecting her, and Rachelle had fallen right into her trap. She'd done exactly what Jolene wanted her to do. Come up here to rescue her mother with nothing but a vase. Slowly, Rachelle brought the glass down to her side. "Please let her go. I beg of you. Let her go."

"You beg of me," Jolene sneered. "You're going to do a lot more than beg before I'm done with you."

Violet whimpered. Her eyes had an edge of hysteria swirling in them. A bruise began to form on her cheek where Jolene had hit her.

"Don't worry, Mom," Rachelle said, not able to bear seeing her mother with such an expression of fear on her face. "Everything's going to be fine."

Jolene tightened her hold and said, "No, everything is

not going to be fine. Not unless I make you go away. And because you didn't die before, now your mom will have to die with you."

"All because I saw you? The sheriff knows what you look like, too. I gave him the pictures. What are you going to do? Kill him, too? And what about the federal agent who's here now? All you're doing is adding more crimes to pay for, and let me make this clear. You *will* be paying for them. All of them, including the hawk. You might as well put the gun down and make things a little easier for yourself."

"Easier? You think things are that black and white? Living on your secluded island all your life has blinded you to reality. You don't have a clue what it's like to live in the real world. I have a boss, and he won't take too kindly if I leave witnesses behind."

"Jolene Almed," a voice from outside spoke on a bullhorn. "We know you're in there. Come out with your hands up."

"See?" Rachelle said. "You're not going to get away with this. They're going to arrest you. You may think our island is backwater, but we don't let criminals get away. My own father was an islander, and they didn't let him get away when he murdered someone. They sure won't let you go."

"They won't catch me. You've got two officers on duty and one fed. There are four sides to the house. They can't be watching all sides. But don't worry. I won't be leaving until I do what I came to do. Get rid of you." With that, Jolene turned the gun on Rachelle and pulled the trigger.

"Shots fired! Shots fired! Caden, do you read? Caden!" Owen's voice carried to Gage's ears as he raced up behind the sheriff, and then right past him.

"Fontaine! Don't you dare go in there!"

Owen's order went ignored as Gage ran up the steps and through the ripped screen door. The front door stood wide open, but he stopped only for the moment it took to hear the commotion and wails coming from upstairs. Female cries followed shouting male's commands.

The federal agent had made it in there. *Thank God!* But had he made it in there in time?

At the top of the staircase, Gage backed up against the wall to approach the bedroom door. Owen came up behind him in silence with his gun drawn and a promise written on his face—*You're a dead man when we're done here*. Gage paid no mind to it. He'd let the sheriff have his way after they got Rachelle out alive.

If she was still alive.

Gage peeked around the door frame. Violet held Rachelle in her arms on the floor at the foot of the bed, weeping over her. Special Agent Caden stood by an open window, white curtains billowing out around him. He placed his drawn gun back into its holster. Had he shot it?

Gage couldn't wonder that for long, because Jolene was nowhere in the room. Had she fallen out the window? Had Caden shot her out? Is that what he was looking at?

Gage didn't care. At the moment, all he cared about was getting to Rachelle. He dropped by her side and saw her eyes wide, but not wide in death. She was still alive. But was she hurt?

"Rachelle." He reached for her face, tapping her cheek to look at him. She was obviously in shock. "Violet, was she shot?"

Violet looked at him but didn't respond. Would she shut down when they needed her most?

"Violet, if you're not going to tell me, then I need you to let go of her so I can check her out."

"I'm okay," Rachelle whispered with a tremble in her voice. Gage wanted to reach for her and take her out of her mother's arms and into his own. But he shouldn't have left her to go to the Underground Küchen in the first place. That had been a big mistake that nearly cost her her life, and he had no right to hold her now.

Violet shook her head and began to speak, slow and weak at first, but quickly strength backed her words. "She didn't get shot. I head-butted Jolene when she aimed the gun at Rachelle. The bullet went that way." Violet pointed to the ceiling where a bullet hole stood out dark against the white plaster. "Then the agent ran in, and Jolene took one look at him and jumped out the window."

Gage glimpsed Caden speaking quietly to Owen. He pushed down on the bill of his cap while he pointed in the direction he saw Jolene go.

The sheriff said as he left the room, "I'll check it out with Baker. She couldn't have gone far. Talk to Gage and tell him what you found out."

Gage nodded to the agent. "Violet," Gage said, and touched the women's hands where she held her daughter tight against her. "Rachelle's safe now. Thanks to you. You did good. Agent Caden needs to speak to me right now. Can you stay with her for a few minutes? I'll be right outside the door. I promise."

"Yes. I don't want to leave her right now." She gripped her daughter tighter.

Gage looked at Agent Caden and stood to meet him at the door. The agent pulled the door closed behind them, but Gage kept his eyes locked where Rachelle lay in her mom's arms even after the door closed.

"She'll be all right. But I can see you care for her. That could be dangerous, you know."

"I know. If Marcus finds out, he'll hurt her just to get to me."

Special Agent Caden nodded in agreement. "I suggest you keep your distance. Maybe find another place to stay."

"I'm working on getting her someplace safe. When Marcus gets here, she'll be nowhere near me. Did you look into what we talked about earlier?" Gage asked in a whisper so as not to be heard.

Agent Caden stood with his arms crossed. "It didn't take me long to look into your story. My sources got back to me with a string of criminal deeds this warlord is responsible for. He could very well be responsible for Pete's death as you think. My sources also tell me, Marcus has left his camp. My guess is he's headed our way, and he'll be here within twenty-four hours."

TEN

"I need to find my boat, Rachelle."

Rachelle heard what Gage wasn't saying.

I need to go.

"You're afraid of Marcus and what he'll do when he gets here." She rested her chin onto the palms of her hands as she leaned on the kitchen table. Gage sat across from her at the little round dinette table. "You've been running for fifteen years from this man. You're tired, but you also want this to end. He's closing in, and you know when he gets here, you're in for the fight of your life. You also know innocent people might die in the melee. Am I getting hot?"

"Smoking." He flashed his bright smile and winked.

She dropped her hands to the table and sat back. "Gage, I'm being serious. Your life is at stake here."

His smile died. "And so is yours. Another incident like the other day can't happen." He bit his lip and looked to be holding something back.

"What's going on? What aren't you telling me?"

"I've made some plans. Your uncle Jerome says you and your mom can go stay with him."

"No." Rachelle shot from her chair, grabbed her breakfast plate and went to wash it vigorously in the sink.

"Just hear me out. If I can get to my ship, I can find the treasure, hopefully before Marcus gets here. It will give me something to bargain with. And it will give me a fighting chance. But I can't leave you alone again. I won't. I shouldn't have left you the other day. Even in the short amount of time I was gone, you weren't safe. If I know you're in a safe place, I can hunt freely. If not your uncle, then how about Len? He's got that secret passage that leads up to his house. Jolene won't know where you are."

"Len." Rachelle whipped around. "You went to see Len? Is that why you went to the Underground Küchen? To talk to them about me? How could you?"

"Rachelle, they care about you." Gage stood from his seat to meet her at the sink. "They love you. They're worried about you, and I know every single one of them would protect you if you would let them."

"Out of pity only."

"No, out of love." He cupped her cheek. "Believe it. They love you. They don't hold you accountable for anything your father did. You can count them as family."

Rachelle gripped his hand as she latched on to his words. "It's not that simple. It's not about them loving me or not."

"Then what's it about? Tell me."

"Why? You can't fix it. You can't fix me."

"Fix you?" Gage scoffed as though he thought she was perfect. If he only knew. "There's nothing wrong with you."

"Maybe not on the outside. But on the inside, I'm horrible. You don't know. I can feel this beast inside of me I don't recognize. It wants to come out and hurt someone. I'm horrible, and I…I know I'm just like my father."

Gage pulled her forehead to his. "No. No you're not. You're your own person with anger and pain inside of you. You've been let down. You feel lost and cast aside from the world you love. That anger inside is a normal reaction."

She rolled her forehead side to side against his. "But

what if I do hurt someone? I would never be able to live with myself."

Gage pulled away and smiled down at her. With both of his hands cupping her cheeks, he leaned down and kissed her forehead. "Rachelle Thibodaux, you are the most gentle person I know. Your love for life and God's creation shows through your pictures. Your desire not to hurt people is stronger than any anger inside of you. I think most people would agree we all have a little monster inside of us rearing to come out. But I think you can feel certain that your desire to not let it come out is stronger."

"You're more certain than I am."

"I'm also certain if you go with me to the Underground Küchen tonight, you will start to let go of some of that anger. Love is a powerful motivator, and when you see how much they love you, I don't think you'll feel as lost anymore."

Rachelle sighed in indecision. "You'll go with me?"

Gage dropped his hands away from her face but covered his heart. "And I promise not to leave your side."

She sighed again. "It is Len's birthday, and I would really like to see him."

"So that's a yes?"

"Everyone from the island will be there."

"Might as well face everyone at once."

"That's not helping." She gritted her teeth in mock annoyance.

Gage smiled bright. "You know, I have to be honest, you're actually really cute when you're mad. Are you sure that's not one those cute pink monsters inside of you? You know, the ones that bake cookies and sing songs?"

Gage stood in the foyer reading the message on the note he'd scrawled out yesterday when he'd finally reached his archeologist associates by phone. With them at sea, he couldn't connect with them sooner, but he needed to tell them to abort the quest for the *Maria's Joy*. When he'd mentioned Marcus had found him, their instructions were clear. Get down to Peru right away. They gave him the co-ordinates and said they would help him lay low. They also mentioned another wreck with emeralds the size of fists waiting for him when he got there. They sure knew what his heart desired.

Gage raised his gaze and caught another pair of emeralds waiting expectantly for him. But these weren't the cold stones he usually sought out. *Joyas radiantes* came to mind as they had the first time he saw her hovering over him. His breath lodged in his throat as Rachelle descended her mom's staircase. Her eyes of radiant jewels reeled him in just as fast as she had the first day she pulled him onto her boat.

Note forgotten, he pocketed it into his jeans and stepped up to offer her a hand down the last step.

"I see you're bringing your camera. I hope it's to take pictures and not to hide behind." He felt a silly smile grow on his lips.

"Both," she said, fingering the strap around her neck.

"Well, at least you're honest." He took in her green sundress with tiny pink flowers. The green matched her eyes perfectly, and before he could control his tongue, he said, "You look beautiful."

"Thank you." She blushed and looked down at her dress. Her dark, silky hair draped down around her shoulders and framed her features when she lifted her face to him again. "It is a step up from my blubber pants."

Gage laughed, but in the end admitted his thoughts about her waders. "If I'm going to be honest, then I have to admit, you look adorable in those, too."

Rachelle scrunched her cute face. "Maybe you're blind."

A giggle came from the living room that caused Rachelle to still.

"Is that you, Mom?"

"Violet's coming, too," Gage informed her.

Rachelle's eyes widened, and turning the corner into the room, she found her mother sitting on the couch with fidgeting hands. "Mom? You're coming out?" Violet nodded slowly, not looking too excited.

"I convinced her it would be safest for you both to stay together with me," Gage informed her from behind. "But my real goal is to see you both back in the community."

Rachelle turned around with a sheen to her eyes that nearly bowled him over. "Thank you, Gage. You've done so much for us. You are truly a good person."

Her praise felt undeserved. His plan to reconnect her with her island family didn't stem from goodness, but rather guilt. He'd brought the danger to her doorstep. Had she forgotten the life he came from? There was nothing good about it.

At the shake of his head, she said, "Don't even try to deny it. Your actions speak louder than your words, mister, and I am so grateful to you." She rushed toward him and threw her arms around him…and caused a jolt of pain to his chest.

"Ouch." He reached between them. "Camera."

Rachelle laughed, stepping back with her hands held tight on his forearms. "I'm so sorry. I wasn't thinking."

He didn't know what bowled him over more. The tears in her eyes or the laughter? His thumbs gently rubbed over her elbows as he wondered what this young woman was doing to him. He was getting too close, and yet, he couldn't let go. The word *love* flashed across his mind like a neon sign, but instantly flickered and went out as he remembered he was unlovable. After all, no one had ever told him otherwise.

He released her in an instant and stepped to the door, picking up her overnight bag she'd packed earlier that day. It was critical to move her into Len's place tonight, but now it was for more reasons than her safety. If he didn't move her tonight, he might be dropping more than danger on her doorstep. He might be dropping his heart.

"You can do this." Gage spoke from beside her at the door to the restaurant, but his words mingled with the ones going on in her head. The ones that told her she had to be crazy for even thinking of going to Len's party with every islander present. Sure, most people would probably be happy to see her and her mom, but there were sure to be people who wouldn't be.

"Promise me if people are vocal about us not being here, we go. Got it?"

Gage huffed. "Sure, but I really don't think you have anything to worry about. In fact, give me the camera, so you don't hurt anyone else when they hug you, because I know they'll want to." He withdrew it from around her neck. "Now, come on, before I change my mind and take you for a stroll on the beach on this warm, breezy evening. I loved nights like this on my boat."

Rachelle smiled. "Sounds wonderful. The boat and the walk. Let's go." She tugged him away from the door.

"Oh, no you don't." He pulled her back. "You have some unfinished business, and I have to see Len about you staying at his house for a little while."

Rachelle blew out a deep breath. "Let's get this over with, then." She breathed deeply again and again.

Gage pulled the door wide, releasing a loud robust ditty she hadn't heard in a year. "They do like to sing here," she mumbled. "We never sang at the Blue Lobster, but secretly, I always wished we did. Just don't tell anyone." She made a shushing sound with her finger to her lips as she passed him and crossed the threshold.

It was as though her shushing had been for everyone in the room. Immediately, the singing stopped, the conversations died down and every head turned to her.

And Rachelle stopped breathing.

Then the smiles began to grow. One by one, Rachelle watched these people who had once been so important to her, and still were, smile just for her.

Slowly, the air returned to her lungs.

"Come, come." Tildy came out from behind the bar. She hugged Rachelle, and then her mom, and then Rachelle again. "I have a seat for you right here in the middle." Tildy led them to Len's table.

"Oh no, Tildy. That's the guest of honor's seat. That's not me. This is Len's party. We came to celebrate him tonight."

"And we celebrate you, too. The lost coin has been found."

"Lost coin?" Rachelle asked the back of her head.

"Yes, just as Jesus said. Suppose a woman has ten silver coins and loses one. Doesn't she light a lamp, sweep the house and search carefully until she finds it? And when she finds it, she calls her friends and neighbors together and says, 'Rejoice with me. I have found my lost coin.' And so we all rejoice here tonight, Rachelle Thibodaux." Tildy turned and cupped her cheek, looking tearfully into Rachelle's eyes. "We have found our precious lost coin." She slapped her cheek lightly. "Now sit. Len, move it."

Len stood and turned to Rachelle. All he had to do was open his arms, and she rushed forward into them. Tears flowed heavily from her eyes, but she didn't care who watched. This man was her grandfather's best friend. He was like a grandfather to her, and to so many.

"There, there," he comforted her. "We have missed you, dear one. But not a day has gone by that we have not prayed for you to come back to us. Tildy is correct. We are rejoicing tonight."

"Happy birthday." Rachelle hugged him one more time and pulled back.

"And what a wonderful gift it is to have you here. Wouldn't you all agree?" Len shouted to the crowd, and cheers erupted from them all. After a few moments, Len stepped away to allow the many who approached them for their turn to hug Rachelle and her mom.

If felt like forever when she finally stood alone with no arms around her. She turned to Gage...and kept turning around.

He was gone. Panic filled her. He'd promised he wouldn't leave her side. Even though most of the people in the room had shown her a warm welcome, she still didn't want to stand here alone. She still wanted him beside her.

Rachelle turned to where Len had sat down, but his chair stood empty. Maybe Gage and Len were speaking in private about her staying with him. Rachelle made her way to the kitchen. No one was in there, but once the swinging doors swung closed behind her, voices could be heard from Len's stairwell. Rachelle stepped up and heard Gage's deep voice. He spoke low, but she would know his suave, charismatic voice anywhere. The deep timbre had a way of calming her nerves and making her smile.

"I made the phone call yesterday," he said. She closed her eyes and let the cadence of his voice work its usual charm. "I've been told to forget about the *Maria's Joy* and get down to Peru."

"When do you leave?" It was Len's voice that brought her back to reality.

Wait. Rachelle's nerves went from calm to tense in less than three seconds. Gage was leaving? Had she heard that right? Her mind raced to retrieve the words he'd just spoken. Something about Peru and forgetting about the *Maria's Joy*. How could he just give up like that? Did this have anything to do with Marcus? How could he let the pirate warlord win?

"I leave as soon as I find my boat. I need to scope out the Peru wreck site and make the grid before the marine archaeologists can bring in their equipment. They say there are emeralds the size of fists. Worth more than the gold and silver here, for sure. If I'd found the *Maria's Joy*, they would have been in Stepping Stones by now. But with the end of summer approaching, the water will be too cold for them to work up here soon. I'd have to find the ship this week to make it work. It's best to abort and move on to warmer waters."

"So, you need Rachelle in a secure place while you hunt your boat down."

"Yes, sir. I'm hoping Marcus will get word I left and follow me away from Stepping Stones. I know he's here. I can feel my skin practically itching under his watchful eye. I expect him to jump out at me at every corner. Rachelle can be nowhere near me when he does. The faster I get out of here the better for her."

"Back to running again, are you? I thought you were done with that."

"If it keeps Rachelle and her island safe, I'll run for the rest of my life."

"No, you won't." Rachelle moved up to the door and started taking the steps. "I won't let you. You're not going anywhere. I'm going to help you find the *Maria's Joy*. I'll even dive if I have to. We can use my boat. The islanders can help with the history of the island to recoup your research and try to piece it all together. Maybe it will tell us where the pirates sunk the ship."

"Dear one." Len spoke when she arrived at the landing they stood on. "I've shown Gage the only thing left here by the pirates." Len pointed his flashlight toward the wall. "He agrees, it doesn't mean anything."

"The Proverbs verse? Let me see your flashlight. I haven't looked at in years, but I also never knew it could be connected to a sunken ship."

Gage touched her hand as she took the flashlight from Len. "Rachelle, I still have to leave. It's best for you if I can lead these pirates away from you. Plus, I'm needed at another job in Peru. There's no time to hunt the *Maria's Joy.* The only boat I need to hunt down is the *Getaway.*"

"So you can *get away?* Funny how Pete named his boat after a successful takedown operation to remind the criminals the navy always wins and no one gets away with breaking the law. But *you,* you use the boat to run away."

Len cackled. "I'm going to leave you two to sort this one out. Son, you've got all our help, just like Rachelle says. What will one more try hurt?" Len left his question hanging there and ambled down the stairs to return to his party.

"Well?" Rachelle clicked on the flashlight. "Shall we? You heard Len. What will one more try hurt?"

"When Marcus shows up here, you'll see how much it hurts." Gage's suave voice didn't have the same calming effect now. Guttural was more like it. She'd even go as far to say pirate-like.

She lowered her voice to match his menacing one. "Then we'd better get started." She passed in front of him to enter the crevice.

Gage erupted behind her. "You don't get it! These are not your hidey-ho pirates with a one-shot pistol and a flimsy compass. These are your Uzi-toting criminals with state-of-the-art tracking equipment. You do not want to be on their radar. Get back here, Rachelle, and listen to me."

She squeezed through the crevice, forgetting how small the space was. She tried to remember the last time she'd come in here and figured she had to have been under twelve. She'd grown a bit since then. At least a little taller, she realized when she bumped her head on the low ceiling.

"When I was younger I used to play in here," she said when she heard Gage squeeze through after her. His deep breathing told her he was fuming mad, but she pretended to be oblivious. "It was my little hideout. I used to imagine being the young woman the pirate was in love with."

She turned to face him, noticing how he curved his back to crouch low. It brought him to her eye level and their lips a breath apart. Rachelle cleared her throat and turned back to the carving to read it. Her throat sounded thick, but she read on.

"'There be three things which are too wonderful for me, yea, four which I know not.'" Rachelle heard Gage grunt beside her. She reached for his hand and twined her fingers through his. "Shh, listen," she whispered, glad to hear her throat was clear again to continue, "'The way of an eagle in the air, the way of a serpent upon a rock, the way of a ship in the midst of the sea—'" She breathed deep and turned to face Gage. Her eyes fell to his lips, still so close as she breathed the last line of the proverb. "'And the way of a man with a maid.'"

Their breathing sounded so loud in the confines of the space. Gage's didn't sound mad anymore. His low growl made him sound tortured, instead. Did he think she would push him away? "Him and me, both," Gage whispered harshly. "'The way of a man with a maid.' I don't understand it, either. Part of me wants to swim out to sea. The other part of me wants to kiss you. But it would put you in so much more danger if Marcus found out how I feel about you. He would hurt you just to get to me."

"How you feel about me?" Her voice squeaked. "How do you feel about me?"

"Confused, tormented and guilt ridden."

"Oh. That doesn't sound very pleasant." She pursed her lips. "I feel like I'm living again. Because of you my feet have found solid ground, and I just want to run with purpose. I want to run into your arms every time you walk into the room to thank you."

"Don't. It could give certain people the wrong idea and put you in danger."

"Again with the danger. I could also be eaten by a shark when I go to work. Or caught in a storm and sent off course. Or I could walk out of here tonight and be shot by Jolene. I could—"

Gage stopped her argument with his strong lips planted firmly on hers.

Rachelle's breath caught in surprise at first, but a moment later she forgot every coherent thought in her mind and melted into him.

But something felt off. No rational thoughts of what it could be came to mind. When he deepened the kiss and held tightly to the sides of her face, she figured it out. She sensed the desperation in him, the need to never let go, and the message became clear.

He would never let this happen again.

Rachelle reached up to pull him closer to her, but the lens of her camera he still wore stood between them. She never thought she would hate her camera, but if she'd known it would be the thing that broke their connection and took him away from her, she would have thrown it out the window.

Gage pulled back, quiet at first, only his breath touching her face in short puffs. She backed away until she couldn't go any farther in the small cavern, her back against the carved wall with the scripture on it. Her knees wobbled, and her hands gripped the cool rock.

She, too, couldn't speak, but she didn't want him to be the first to break the silence with apologies or promises to never let that happen again. She knew he felt responsible for the danger she was in. The least she could do was let him off easy for caving now. She pressed her fingertips to her lips where she still felt his touch and memorized the sensation for always. "Don't worry, I won't tell anyone. Whatever you do, don't apologize. It was special to me, and I want to keep it that way." She gouged the fingers of her other hand into the rocks, waiting for him to reply. Her thumb touched something with a different texture than the rest of the rock wall. Some type of object was imbedded in the wall.

"I need to leave, Rachelle," Gage said into the darkness. She must have dropped the flashlight at her feet during their kiss. Which worked out fine now. She would much rather leave them in the dark while he spoke of leaving her forever. She didn't want him to see her face crumple at the idea of parting ways. "I'll never find the treasure in time. It's best that I find my boat and keep any more trouble from broaching your shores."

She gripped the wall tighter as tears sprang to her eyes. Her thumb hit the foreign object in the wall again and drew her attention away from Gage's farewell. Whatever lay beneath her thumb piqued her curiosity, but she would need the flashlight to identify it.

She bent to retrieve the light and found the contrasting part of the wall again. "Gage, what is this?" She pried at something thin that shone golden in the flashlight.

"Hold the light, and let me see," he instructed as he bent to study the object. "It looks like the side of a coin wedged in a small crevice. My wide fingers won't retrieve it. Do you have a pin in your hair? Maybe I can pick it out."

"No, but let me think. Um… Oh, how about the photo card in my camera? That's thin and might fit in the opening enough to push out the object."

"Worth a shot," he said as he opened the compartment to retrieve the small, thin memory card.

A few pokes and a gold coin popped out. Gage caught it before it slipped to the floor and rolled away.

"Is there a date on it?"

"Yeah, and I don't believe it," he said in an awed hush. "It's 1726."

"Wow, that's got to be worth a fortune. It's in perfect condition."

"That's because it was brand-new when it was put in here, fresh off the boat from Spain."

"Spain? Wasn't the *Maria's Joy* from Spain?"

"Yes, and even without my research notes, I can positively say this coin was part of her manifest. Meaning it was part of her precious cargo."

"Gage, you know what this means, don't you? The *Maria's Joy* is here on Stepping Stones just like you thought. Her final resting place is right here in our waters. We can find her."

Gage stood as high as the ceiling would allow him, once again at her eye level. "No. I'm no closer to finding her than I was five minutes ago. This mission has been aborted. It's over."

"But what about the scripture? Seeing that the coin is here, this scripture must tell you where the ship is. The carver put the coin here as a clue."

Gage cupped the back of her head and pulled her forehead. "Let it go, Rachelle. Please."

"No," she said, and pulled away. "I can help you. I can figure this out."

"It's too late. Time is ticking. A sheriff, a deputy and a federal agent will not keep Marcus at bay. You'll never forgive yourself if one of the islanders gets hurt. And I'll never forgive myself if you get hurt."

Rachelle bit her lip as she studied the wall. She whispered the lines over and over, trying to make sense of them. "The eagle. The eagle. An eagle in the air. The hawks! I know where the hawks are. It's harsh terrain. You can't get there by car. Only by boat. I have to be really careful when I go there. There's a lot of rocks. Rocks! Rocks and serpents. Snakes! Snake on a rock. That's it! That's where she is. That's where you'll find a ship in the midst of the sea. Gage, we found her! She's on that side of the island."

"Wait. Just wait. We haven't found anything yet. A boat does not sink on dry land."

"No, but maybe that's what the rest of the clue is. The way of a man with a maid."

"How is the way of a man with a maid a clue to a sunken ship? What does that mean?"

"I don't know. You tell me. What does it mean?" Somehow it didn't feel that they were speaking about the treasure anymore. "How does a man think of a young woman?"

"Easy. She's a treasure to protect and to hold in his heart forever."

Rachelle dropped her gaze to Gage's chest. She curled her fingers in to stop from placing her hand over his heart. Would he hold her in his heart forever? But that would imply she was a valuable treasure worth protecting and keeping there. "All I ask is that you give me one chance to follow this lead." She swallowed hard. "Then you can leave."

Gage exhaled deep and long. "If anything happened to you—"

"Nothing can happen to me with you by my side. We're doing this together."

"And where do you suppose we start?"

"We start where the eagles fly and the snakes crawl on the rocks. We start on Emerald Point."

Gage sputtered in the dark. "I'm sorry, what did you say? Did you say *Emerald* Point?"

"Yes, that's what that part of the island is called. So, are you on board? Do we start tomorrow morning?"

His lips curled in the beam of light. "How can I say no? I've never been able to say no to emeralds."

ELEVEN

"Good morning." Rachelle stepped out of Len's passageway and met Gage in the kitchen of the restaurant. She caught him with a bite of Tildy's amazing strudel in his mouth. "Good, huh?" Rachelle smiled and waited for him to finish on a gulp.

He wiped the corners of his mouth. "Unbelievably good. I might have to kidnap her when I set sail. I could use a good cook on board."

Rachelle's cheerful smile evaporated in an instant. He knew she held out hope that he might stay on Stepping Stones, but that was one commitment he couldn't make. "Rachelle, I live at sea. You know this."

"Only because you've never had a home on land. The whole island loves you." She stopped there, but he wondered if she had been about to say that she loved him. Friendship shone from her eyes, but that didn't mean love. Nobody had ever told him they loved him, and the selfish part of him that hoped she'd be the first unsettled him. Proof he needed to create some distance between them, not spend more time with her looking for a sunken ship. This was a bad move all around.

He could never live on land, and she could never live at sea. He couldn't imagine how low her spirits would become after days with nothing but water surrounding her. No animals to photograph. No life at all. Diving scared her, so marine life photography wasn't an option. Seafaring would be a miserable existence. He would be dropping another death tank on someone's shoulders. No. He wouldn't do that again. He could never ask her to join him at sea.

If she would even want to.

She'd admitted their kiss had been special, that she was feeling alive again. But that didn't constitute love. That meant God was waking her up from her self-imposed slumber. Watching the change in her since he arrived on the island proved God was working on her. He was lifting her from the rock bottom she'd been on this past year.

"Gage, haven't you ever wanted a family?"

Her question caught him off guard. "Pete was my family. He was an older brother and father all rolled into one."

"Did he boss you around like an older brother?" Her green eyes sparkled with her teasing mirth.

Gage shrugged. "I suppose we had our moments. It would be hard to spend day and night on a boat with someone and not get on each other's nerves."

She frowned. "Agent Caden thinks someone killed him. That his death wasn't an accident. What do you think?"

"I think we should be going if we're going to make the service."

"Service? What service? What are you talking about? I thought we were going treasure hunting."

"We are, but first we're going to church."

"Church? I haven't been to church in over a year. I can't just show up."

"Sure you can, and God's not counting any of the days you missed."

"Maybe God's not, but everyone else is."

"Rachelle, you saw most everyone last night. They were

excited to see you. They've welcomed you back home. They want you to be a part of the family again."

"This coming from someone who doesn't even belong to a church."

"That's my point, church isn't a building. God has called us to be the church all over the world. I take that literally, and whenever I'm in port, I find a place to worship with my Christian family. I've worshipped openly in cathedrals, and I've worshipped secretly in basements. You're blessed to have a stone-and-mortar building to come together and worship freely. Don't take it for granted and don't be the missing member of the family."

"What about my mom?" Rachelle let Gage pull her to the door, but before he opened it to step out, he held her back to scan up and down the boardwalk.

"Okay, it looks safe." Gage frowned. "I already asked her. She said she wasn't ready yet. It wasn't a *no,* though. I'm still praying for her. It won't be long now, I'm sure."

Rachelle's feet slowed on the wooden boards. "You pray for my mom?"

He grabbed her hand and tugged. "You have to be a little faster out here. It's not safe to stand around. Jolene could be hiding behind any one of these little store shacks. And I'm sure Marcus has arrived and is lurking, too, waiting for his most opportune moment to strike."

"Then what are we doing out here? Let's get to my boat and get over to the other side of the island."

"I'm not thinking Jolene's near here right now. She and Marcus are probably out at sea making a plan."

"What kind of plan?"

He draped his arm around her shoulders when a breeze picked up off the sea. "Did you think to bring a windbreaker? That storm that's been brewing at sea this week looks like it might make a run for land today."

"I have a raincoat on the boat. But you didn't answer my question. What kind of plan are they making?"

They arrived at a little white church with green shutters. "Not now. We'll talk later. The music is starting." He led the way up the short staircase and opened the green wooden door. A flood of piano notes poured a hymn. He tugged and before she could take a deep breath, they were inside and the door behind her closed on a bang.

The whole congregation turned around with hymnals in hand.

Gage raised his hands. "I'm so sorry. It's getting windy out there." As heads faced forward again, he mouthed, *Oops,* to Rachelle and ushered her into the last pew.

He opened a hymnal for them both to share and proceeded to pray silently for her safety in whatever developments occurred today. Her dark head of hair leaned close to read the words on the page while Gage closed his eyes. *Please God, I ask for Your protection over her from whatever danger is blowing in today. Rachelle asked about the plans Marcus and Jolene were making, but the truth is I can't imagine the kinds of torture they have in mind. Help me, Lord, to find my boat, so I can lead Marcus away from here for good. Help me to take this evil man as far away from here as possible. And, thank You for Owen and Special Agent Caden's help in ending my days of running. Help me during this crucial time. But through whatever transpires, I pray for Your help in keeping my eyes on You the whole time, and I pray Rachelle realizes how important she is to You.*

The music ended, and Rachelle closed the book to replace it in the pew rack. She grabbed his hand, pulling his attention to her. Her head tilted in concern. "It's bad, isn't it?" she whispered. "What they're planning is going to be bad. I can see the worry on your face."

"We'll make it through." They took their seats for the pastor to speak, but Gage's heart ached for how Rachelle viewed herself. Gage lifted his eyes to the pastor to listen carefully to the message, but as he took in the backs of everyone's heads, one head turned around to face him.

Deputy Baker.

The man was dressed in his uniform and sat with his girlfriend. Gretchen, if Gage remembered correctly. Gage nodded to the deputy but received no reply.

The pastor mentioned failed escapes and old strategies that didn't work. He took Gage's attention away from the deputy, but soon the pastor's voice blurred in with Gage's thoughts. He could have no failed escapes today. Rachelle's life depended on it. And so did his.

Something deep inside Gage stirred. His days of running were at an end. Running was an old strategy that never worked. But Gage had to wonder why he'd allowed fifteen years of it. Was it in fear of his life? Or fear of losing his boat?

His home.

The only home he'd ever had.

What would his life mean if he lost his boat forever?

He'd told Rachelle God was looking for her because she was valuable to Him, but every time she brought his past up, he covered it up by saying his boat was his home...as though it was his boat that gave him value. It was an old strategy that kept the pain of never having a home at bay. Of never facing the truth and the pain. As long as he had the *Getaway,* he had a place to belong.

Or maybe hide away on.

As long as he believed that it was his boat that gave him value and not God's love in his life, he would be running.

Even running from God.

Gage bowed his head, shaking it and praying over and

over again. *No, God. I don't want anything to come between us. I don't want to hide from You or run from You. You are my home.*

Rachelle shook his shoulder. "Gage. Gage, the service is over. You ready to go?"

He heard her words, but much like the rest of the service, they were a blur to the words moving around in his head. No more failed escapes. There would be no more running. The old strategies were done. He would face the truth head on, and he would face it with God at his side, not in his wake.

"Let's go. We have a treasure to find and a past to face." He grabbed her hand and headed to the door. Most of the people had left or mingled out on the front walkway.

A group clustered at the base of the stairs. One was Baker's girlfriend, Gretchen. The other was another woman in her thirties. A beautiful redhead with a soft smile. When she lifted her hands and began to use sign language, Gage realized she was deaf. To his surprise, Rachelle answered her with her hands, as well. He had no idea she knew sign language. This woman astounded him. There was so much she kept hidden behind that mask of hers.

"Gage, this is Miriam Matthews, the sheriff's wife." Rachelle stepped up beside Miriam. "She's the school's principal, too. She can read lips a little. Miriam says she's had the federal agent's company at her home this week, when he's been there that is, which hasn't been much because he's been out searching for Jolene. But as you know Stepping Stones doesn't have lodging for him to stay anywhere else."

Gretchen piped up, "Not for long. I'm thinking of opening a B and B."

"Really, Gretchen?" Rachelle said. "That's great. Where about?"

As the two old friends chatted, Miriam reached for Gage's hand and held it for a few moments. The blowing wind swirled her golden-red hair around her face, but her granite-gray eyes locked on him as though she searched for an answer to some question only she knew. "My husband says you are in danger," she said.

Gage shrugged her remark off. "Danger I brought here with me, but I'm going to end it today."

Miriam shook her head, her eyes squinting. Had he spoken too fast for her to understand? She started signing real fast. He was lost and looked to Rachelle for interpretation, but her look of concern had him holding off. What was Miriam saying?

"Where are you two off to today?" Deputy Baker came out of nowhere and stepped up beside his girlfriend.

Gage dragged his attention from the woman signing to look at the deputy. The man draped an arm around his girlfriend and pulled her close to his side, quite territorial like, but Gage held his tongue. He also wasn't up for sharing their treasure-hunting plans for the day, but then figured the sheriff's department should know where they were going in case something happened. "We're going out in the lobster boat to someplace called Emerald Point."

"Emerald Point can be kind of dangerous. Especially if a storm blows in. Those rocks get covered up real fast. You might want to pay attention to the skies if you head over there."

"We will, but, Rachelle, we'd better move it if we want to have time to look around."

Rachelle had her lower lip between her teeth, concern flooding her eyes. She nodded and gave Miriam a quick hug. Baker's girlfriend smiled, but didn't step up to hug Rachelle. But then she really couldn't with the way Baker had her locked in his grip. Rachelle gave her a little wave and fell into step beside him as they made their way to the docks.

"What was Miriam talking to you about back there?" he asked when they were far enough away.

"Nothing really. Miriam's just a real good judge of character. That's what makes her a good principal. She's very intuitive with people. She wanted to make sure you knew you're just as important as everyone else. And she wanted to make sure you didn't feel guilty about bringing the danger here."

"Well, that's nice of her, but does she realize her husband's life is at risk because of me? She could be a widow by nightfall. It's a good thing Owen has Caden as backup. Baker is useless. Speaking of which, what is up with him and his girlfriend? Are they that close, or is he holding on awfully tight?"

"I don't know. Gretchen used to be my best friend. At one time, she might have shared with me but not since my dad was arrested. Billy wanted the job as deputy and didn't think it would look good for his girlfriend to be hanging with the jailbird's daughter."

Gage pulled her close to his side to rub her shoulder. "That's ignorance. Don't take it personally."

"How can I not? Gretchen listened to him." Rachelle sighed and continued, "But then, I also didn't make it easy for people to find me. I did a lot of hiding."

"Well, that makes two of us. What do you say we both stop doing that and go free some treasure from its hiding place, too?"

Rachelle picked up her step with a big grin in agreement. "Emerald Point, here we come."

"So, why is this side of the island called Emerald Point?" Gage asked Rachelle as he pulled the port side up to a huge rock they could use as a makeshift dock. "All I see are a bunch of rocks and cliffs."

She dropped anchor and held the wheel to stand steady in the rocking waves. "As far as I know, the pirates named it. It sounds pretty, so I guess the name stuck." She grabbed her camera. "We'd better get started. These waves are crazy. We don't want to get stranded here if the storm comes in. This whole area will be under water."

"After you." Gage offered his arm for her to step up and over the side of her boat to the rock beside it. He joined her right after, and together they headed inland, crunching on loose rocks and climbing up and over larger ones. "I can see where Stepping Stones gets its name."

"There are a lot of submerged rocks that surround the island, too, but nothing like the treacherous ones near Emerald Point. A ship has to be real careful sailing in close to this side of the island."

"Including an old Spanish galleon. The *Maria's Joy* could have been sunk by any one of these boulders."

"Our best chance to find out which one did the deed will be to go up." Rachelle pointed to the top of a cliff. "That's where I took the pictures of the hawk."

"You've scaled that thing? You are full of surprises today. First, you speak sign language, now you scale cliffs."

Rachelle laughed. "I don't scale cliffs. There's a path that rounds up the back." She pointed the way and started up the embankment. "I may be good at tying knots, but only for fishing, not for hoisting myself up the side of rock walls."

"What about the sign language?" he called from behind.

"I'm not good at that, either, but I practice as much as I can, especially when Miriam comes to see me, even though I'm the last person she should want to be around."

"Why's that?"

"She was nearly my father's second victim." Rachelle stopped and turned around. What kind of expression would be on his face? Would he finally be repulsed by her?

He wore a frown but not revulsion. It also wasn't pity like the expression of so many islanders. "Your father has caused a lot of pain. Sometimes we make choices in our lives that benefit us but hurt the ones we love. We can hope we'll make the right choice that will put others first, but that isn't always the case. One thing is for sure, though— they are our choices and no one else's. You should never feel responsible for the decision of someone else."

"I don't feel responsible, but I've had to pay for it like I am. I don't think you get it." She shook the conversation off and turned away to walk on. The path grew less rocky and narrow as she stepped into a forest of pine trees. Fallen needles covered the path, and tree roots reached across in places. "Careful up here. This path is filled with high roots. A lot of places to trip and fall flat on your face." She turned back around to find the path empty. "Gage? Where are you?" Her voice cracked as her breath caught in her throat.

Rachelle took a few steps back down the path. Had she walked too fast and left him behind? Had her brush-off to his words been the last straw?

Or had something horrible happened to him?

She half expected to find him facedown, taken out by a sharp shooter. A scan of the cliffs above came up empty and allowed her to pick up her steps, but before she walked three more feet, Gage jumped out from behind a tree.

Rachelle shrieked and threw up her arms in front of her. Flaps of multiple birds' wings shook the trees above them as her shout echoed out in sound waves. "Why would you scare me like that?" she demanded of his grinning face.

Gage's shoulders shook with laughter, and the next moment he scooped her up in his arms.

"Put me down!" Rachelle shouted and pummeled his chest. "What are you doing?"

"I'm treating you to an afternoon of carefree living."

"Right, because you're a pro at that type of lifestyle. That's what all your afternoons are like."

"Don't knock it until you've tried it. And I do have a job, you know. I may not sit at a desk all day, but I work hard for my living."

"Diving for buried treasure sounds like a little kid's daydream, not a job."

"Jealous?"

"Yes," Rachelle said begrudgingly, but with each of his steps up the slope, her lips cracked into a smile. He winked back at her, looking himself like an old pirate. "It must be nice to live day to day with no schedule to keep. No problems to solve. If I show up late to work, I have cannibalistic crustaceans to deal with."

"That's where you're wrong. If I show up late for work, I have competitors stealing my profits. Word gets out that I'm heading to a certain destination, and before you know it, every treasure hunter in the hemisphere is circling the waters. Time is critical. If I find the wreck, I file all the necessary paperwork to be the sole custodian and exclusive salvager. That prohibits anyone from entering a zone a mile in diameter around the site. If they enter, I can get a federal arrest warrant for violating my custody. So you see, my little skeptic, I, too, have paperwork. It's not all lazing around on deck in the afternoon sun like you seem to think."

"Oh, poor you. You have to fill out a form. Is that all?"

He stepped out into the clearing. Another twenty steps and they would stand at the cliff's edge with the wide-open

sea before them. "No, that's not all. Before I ever get to
that point, before I ever even set sail, I've spent countless
hours scouring old documents, newspaper articles, local archives, books, testimonies, churches, any place that might
direct me to a wreck site. Monasteries, especially, offer
great archives. There was usually a clergyman on board a
ship, especially the Spanish boats. It was their job to write
things down. The only reason I know about the *Maria's
Joy* being in the area was because she had a sister ship that
traveled with her. The pirates stole the *Maria's Joy,* but the
Buen Rosa, the *Good Rosa* got away. It was documented
that the stolen ship sailed north following the North Atlantic Drift. It was seen in Massachusetts before sailing
farther north, said to have been heading to Pirate Island.
And that is what brings me here today."

Rachelle had stilled in his arms, subdued by the deep
cadence of Gage's voice as he spoke, but also by the pure
contentment emanating from his composure and expres-
sive eyes. He loved what he did for a living. And by the
sounds of it, it was a job.

"I'm sorry," she said.

"For what?" His face leaned in close to hers, a slight
smile to his lips. The same lips she knew so personally
now and would remember always.

"For not respecting your career. I was wrong. I had no
right to judge the way you earned a living. It's a job to be
proud of."

"Thank you, but I will admit, I have my lazy afternoons,
too." He grinned. "And mornings, too, for that matter."
His eyes grew wide. "Oh, Rachelle, you should see the
mornings. They are amazing. The way the lavender sky
smudges into soft pinks and tangerines. You could take a
million photos and never capture it the same way twice."

"I don't usually photograph the sun. I typically stick with wildlife."

"Right." His eyes dulled along with his smile. Slowly, he brought her feet to the hard ground and broke the connection they shared. A cold wind whipped between them.

"Did I say something wrong?" she asked.

He shook his head and reached for her hand to head to the cliff's edge. "You have a special talent, Rachelle. You bring pictures to life. Your love for God's creatures shines through with every image you take. I hope someday you'll find a way to make a living at it. Have you ever thought of photojournalism? I've worked with a few photographers, under the sea of course, but you could stay on dry land."

Rachelle bit her lower lip. The glimpse into the life Gage spoke of was intriguing. "But that would mean leaving Stepping Stones. My mom needs me. I couldn't leave here so easily."

"Maybe you're not giving your mom enough credit. She's not an invalid, and I've seen a fresh spark of life in her eyes. I think she's coming around."

"Because of you. You've been so great to her. Thank you, Gage. I don't know how I can ever thank you."

"Take our picture."

"What? That's hardly repayment for all you've done."

"It's all I want. Something to take with me."

Rachelle refused to frown even though the edges of mouth had a will of their own. She fought against the twitching muscles as she lifted her camera from her chest. "I need a rock or something to set this on. I think there's one on the other side of the cliff, through those trees." She nodded her head in the direction. Gage turned, giving her a reprieve in hiding her disappointment.

He led the way with her at his strong back. So close she walked, thinking very soon she would be left behind with his back to her forever. *Gage, I think I'm falling in love with you.*

The words sat on her tongue wanting to spill from her mouth like fish from a net. There was no holding them back. Slippery little words with minds of their own.

The wind tumbled his hair at his neck, making her wish her fingers were the wind. He moved with each step as though he was part of the land. She nearly reached out to touch him, but they came to the flat rock she remembered being here. The ledge was only a few feet away. "Careful standing on the edge. I don't want you to fall."

"You, either," he said as she set the timer on her camera.

"Ten seconds. Nine." Rachelle stepped up beside him, unsure of where to put her hands. "Eight. Seven." She left them folded down in front of her. "Six. Five. Four. Three."

Gage encircled her with both his arms, laying his chin on top of her head. Her hands immediately reached up to hold on to his forearm at her front. Her eyes closed as she melted into his embrace.

The camera clicked, but neither of them moved. The wind whipped hard. Standing at this precipice, she felt as if it would blow them over the edge. She had no strength to fight it if it did.

Rachelle turned to face Gage, her arms wrapping through his and up over his shoulders. She pulled tight and pushed her cheek in, her ear covering the place his heart beat at a rapid pace as she stared out to sea. His hands cupped the back of her head. His fingers twined through her hair, lulling her like the wind fluttering her eyelashes, drying the tears forming there.

Waves crashed below against the many rocks, over and over like they had done for centuries. These very same rocks were the rocks the pirates had navigated nearly three hundred years ago. Some of them long and flat, others jutted up out of the sea, eroded and formed into various shapes and peaks, like hearts and diamonds.

A profound crack in one of the heart-shaped rocks reminded her how her own heart felt broken at the thought of Gage leaving forever. "I'm really going to miss you," she admitted with nothing else to lose.

He gently lifted her chin to face him. "I'm going to miss you, too." Before she knew what he planned, he brushed his lips across hers in a soft touch that spread warmth through her body, combating the whipping wind and her deep sadness. It ended too soon, but when he pulled away, he wore his signature grin. Apparently the kiss did the same for him. "But I'm not gone yet," he reminded her. "So what do you say you grace me with your beautiful smile and help me find a sunken treasure?"

"Like you grace me with yours? Tell me, Gage, when do you not have a smile on your face? I can't imagine you any other way."

He flashed his pearly whites wide. "A cheerful heart is good medicine, but a crushed spirit dries up the bones. And speaking of bones, we have the bones of a ship to find. Where those bones lie is where we will find the gold and silver. So where is this Emerald Point you're taking me to?"

Rachelle reluctantly stepped out of his arms and thumbed over her shoulder as she reached for her camera. "Through those woods a little way. You come out to another ledge where it jets out to a point. It's really steep and narrow. It's also where the hawk's nest is." She frowned. "Of course, now the nest will be empty. You can climb out pretty close to it, but I'm not sure if I want to see it."

Gage stepped up to her. He pressed his lips to her forehead and sighed. "I'm sorry. I know the bird meant a lot to you. But please remember how vengeance can be yours.

It's not in retaliation. It's in victory. And you will have victory. I promise. Now, come on, let's see what Emerald Point points us to."

Gage led Rachelle through the trees and heavy covering of pine needles. Squirrels and chipmunks sprang out of their hiding places to race up the many tree trunks. They came to a wide-open field, filled with rocks mixed with tall, wavy grasses. But just as Rachelle had described, the field inclined, gradually at first, then at sharp intervals until the land elevated to a ledge overlooking the sea.

Emerald Point.

At this far distance, Gage didn't see a speck of green to warrant such a name. "Stay here. I want to see what it might be pointing at. It doesn't look wide enough out there for both of us."

"It's not, but—"

A high-pitched screech echoed through the sky above. The sound made Gage duck and cover his head, but not Rachelle.

One second she stood in front of him, and the next, she flew past him in the direction of the point. "A hawk!" she shouted. "It's a hawk!"

Gage looked to the sky but saw no bird of prey above him. He circled around, knowing it had to be here somewhere. He'd heard it, and the hair on the back of his neck still stood at attention from its hunting shrill.

Rachelle reached the incline, and her steps grew shorter and more deliberate as the land narrowed.

"Be careful!" Gage yelled, and followed her. She stopped when she couldn't go any farther, and just as he reached the incline, she turned and waved her hand to hurry him up.

"It's a female!" she whispered loudly to be heard in the wind and waves. "He had a mate!"

In the next moment, a large hawk swooped up from the opposing side of the ledge. Gage feinted back in the surprise and crouched to his knees. After the initial shock, the experience turned to wonder and amazement. The bird's wings spread wide in majesty. The tail fanned out in a beautiful array of reds.

Rachelle's camera clicked repeatedly.

"You're getting this?" he asked in a hushed tone.

"You bet I am," she answered, but her complete focus was through her camera's lens. More clicks set off in rapid sequence. Then the bird came in for a landing somewhere above.

"Is that where the nest is? Up there?"

"Yes, you want to see?" She waved him on past her. "Hold the rocks tight."

A few times he slipped when the rocks crumbled down far below him. "I thought you said you weren't a rock climber."

"Shh, don't scare her," Rachelle said from behind as she searched through her photos. "Oh, these are great," she mumbled to herself, oblivious to the fact he'd almost met his death.

Gage climbed a few more rocks and leaned to his left, coming so close to the edge that sweat broke on his forehead and palms. He searched ahead for the nest, but a black flag waving in the wind halted his search, and nearly stopped his beating heart.

Scrawled across the flag was Psalm 18:16.

The flag flapped from the mast of a yacht. He didn't need to go any farther to know he'd found his boat.

Gage scrambled backward down the rocks until he could find sure footing. "How do I get down there?" He rushed his question out, not wanting to wait for an answer. He wanted to go now.

"Why? What's going on? What did you see?"

"My boat. Tell me how to get down there."

Rachelle jumped to her feet, biting her lip. "Um…I'm not sure you can get there from here. I'm not even sure you can get there with my boat. The rocks are too close together. You might have to swim."

"There must be some place to get through, because Jolene has it anchored right below the ledge. I have to go." He took off back toward the trees.

"Wait, what if it's a trap? I don't think you should go alone. If you won't wait for help, then at least let me go with you." Rachelle raced after him, catching up to his pace.

"No!" He stopped to grab her arms. "It's not safe. I am not bringing you to Jolene like some gift. In fact, I want you to get to your boat and radio Sheriff Matthews and Special Agent Caden. Tell them what's going on. They'll know what to do. Then go home, Rachelle. Do you hear me? Go home."

Gage left her and picked up his step to a breakneck speed. He'd found his boat. This changed everything. He could leave. He could force the danger away from Stepping Stones and away from Rachelle.

He passed the ledge they'd stood at a little while ago for their photo. He didn't even get to look at the picture, but he didn't have to, to know the expression on his face. And the tears he sealed tight between his lids.

He would miss her so much. But birds lived on the land, and fish lived in the sea. They could never be more to each other. Where would they live? How would they breathe?

At least here she would be alive.

Gage came barreling down the last path and reached the shoreline. The cliff stretched out into the sea. Rachelle was right. He would need to swim to get around it. There must be an inlet on the other side, and Jolene had found a way to navigate in without brushing against the rocks. He hoped anyway. She very well could have wrecked the *Getaway* and left it for salvage.

Except, she'd have some explaining to do to her boss. Marcus would be irate if she damaged the boat he wanted. Jolene wouldn't risk a penalty just for spite. The woman was smart. Gage figured she'd most likely been gentle and cautious when she hid the boat in the inlet.

He supposed he could try to take Rachelle's boat in, but if he damaged her boat, he'd put her out of commission.

He'd have to swim.

Gage pushed through the rough waves until water reached his thighs. The water's strength nearly plowed him over. The storm was not far-off. He could see the swells smashing into the side of the cliff. It would be about a thousand yards before he reached the inlet, but he had to do it. There could be no turning back now. Victory hung so close.

Gage raised his arms and dived into a freestyle swim stroke that would have taken him faster if not for the rushing waves and the clothes on his back. His body weakened against the mighty sea. Each stroke stole more of his energy. At this rate, he'd lose the battle before he boarded the boat. Gage lifted his face only to have a wave pelt him and leave him sputtering. A huge rock successfully tempted him to grab on and rest.

He breathed and scanned the horizon. A rock shaped like a split heart grabbed his attention. Man, he had it bad for Rachelle, if he was seeing broken hearts in the sea.

Gage shook his head and dropped back into the water to swim the rest of the way. He reached the entrance to the thin inlet. From the entrance he couldn't see his boat and was surprised Jolene had been able to get through the opening—and far enough in that a boat passing by couldn't see it. No wonder no one could find her. Owen had sent a message to the coast guard to be on the lookout, but no response came back. That was because she was hidden in here.

Gage swam through the entrance, sticking close to the cliff and low in the water. Only his eyes and nose emerged from the water as he quietly moved in. He didn't need Jolene taking shots at him before he reached his boat.

The water quieted the farther in he swam. The inlet curved to the left, and then just as Gage turned the corner, the *Getaway* emerged into his view.

He felt his chest rumble in the water as he let out a low *Thank you, Jesus*. Home sweet home. Gage's heart sped up along with his arms and legs. Her navy-blue hull looked beautiful, at least from this side. No damage from what he could see. Her sails were closed up neatly, and she looked well cared for. He would thank Jolene…*after* she'd been arrested.

Gage wasn't against justice. The criminal system was in place to protect the innocent from people who meant them harm. Jolene had meant Rachelle harm and needed to pay for her crimes. Her crimes also included stealing his boat. Yes, she worked under Marcus's orders, but she didn't have to. If she exercised her free will in a criminal manner, then she would pay for it in the system set up for such choices.

He hoped she didn't add on more crimes when he attempted to reclaim his boat. But just in case, he wouldn't be shouting *Honey, I'm home!* He'd enter through the opening where his small launch boat traveled and where the dive platform at the boat's aft was low enough for him to board with quiet stealth and ease.

He was reminded of the last time he snuck on the *Getaway,* fifteen years ago when he planned to commandeer the ship from Pete. That had been a fight to the near death.

Today would be no different.

Gage lifted his upper body out of the water and lay flat on the dive platform but only for the second it took him to pull his legs out of the water. He raced forward, out of the viewing area from above. He squeezed the dripping water from his shirt and shorts before moving forward to a portal on the other side of his launch boat. Glad to see it unlocked, he entered a silent hallway and observed any movements from above.

Not a sound. The whole boat was at rest. Did that mean Jolene wasn't here? But if she wasn't here, where was she?

A sick feeling filled his core. He'd left Rachelle alone. Had Jolene used his boat as a trap so she could go after Rachelle? If so, he had to return right away.

Gage reached for the handle in the same moment the floor creaked above him. His hand froze in its tight grip.

Jolene was on board. Gage dropped his hand to his side as he realized that meant Rachelle was safe. For now.

Breathing came easier, and Gage took one deep inhale and inched toward the stairs to carry out his original mission.

Get his boat back. Then get back to Rachelle.

The door to his engine room remained closed, and as Gage passed by, he tensed in preparation of someone exiting. He passed without any excitement and made his way to the stairs. Placing his feet lightly on the treads, he took them without a sound. At the top step, he unclicked the latch to open the door. The salon could be seen through the opening.

His maps and research scattered every flat surface. The plush blue fabric of the bench seating could barely be seen beneath the papers. The single-legged table that the seating surrounded had a map of Stepping Stones for a tablecloth.

It would appear Jolene had been treasure hunting.

Had she found the *Maria's Joy?*

Gage pushed the door a little wider to peer beyond the salon into the galley kitchen. Both rooms stood empty. But Jolene was up here. She'd walked across the floor and made it creak.

He pushed the door wide enough for him to fit and stepped into the salon. If she had been here before, it didn't sound like she was now.

Gage looked beyond the couches to the covered exterior deck. Above him was the captain's stateroom and guest stateroom. The small study to his right led to the head. Jolene could be slinking behind either of those closed doors.

A few steps inside the salon, Gage caught a glance of some markings on his map. A red circle around the place he knew to be called Emerald Point. Right where they were, and right where she'd moored his boat. So she hadn't put his boat here just to hide it. She knew the treasure was in the vicinity.

The door to the study opened behind, but Gage kept his back to her. "So, tell me, Jolene, have you found the *Maria's Joy?*" Gage turned to face her, but before he could, pain splintered through his head, the force sprawling him across the table and map and into a black oblivion.

TWELVE

Rachelle made it to her lobster boat and launched herself across the deck for the radio. Her camera swung out and clipped the wheel with a crack. She cringed, but it would have to wait until after she made contact with Owen, though. Help for Gage was the priority.

"Owen! Do you read?" Pain ripped from her lower lip where her teeth penetrated through the skin. "Owen!"

Her radio crackled, before a voice came over the speaker. "This is Deputy Baker. What is your emergency?"

"Billy!" Rachelle rushed forward. "This is Rachelle. I'm over at Emerald Point. We found Gage's boat hidden in the inlet. Can you tell the sheriff to come quickly? Jolene needs to be arrested. Now!"

Silence returned. Not a sound of any voice or crackling.

"Billy, did you hear me?"

"Yup, I heard. Sheriff Matthews is tied up right now. In case you're just getting on board with the situation, we have a warlord broaching our shores. Sheriff Matthews has been on the phone with the Portsmouth naval base all morning requesting surveillance for an unidentified vessel. He's on the phone with the feds now. This is big-time, and Gage's boat is the least of our worries."

"But Jolene needs to be stopped before she hurts anyone else."

The radio crackled for a split second before Deputy Baker said, "I'll come check it out, but only because I'm well aware of who needs to be stopped, and Jolene isn't the only one."

Rachelle scrunched her eyes at the radio. "What is that supposed to mean?" she spoke into the radio with a little edge to her voice.

"I mean the company you keep is a reflection of who you are. I shouldn't be surprised you'd go for a criminal. Like father like daughter. Are you aware of how the *Getaway*'s previous captain died? Did you know it wasn't an accident?"

Rachelle bit her tongue to stop her from shouting at the radio. She took a deep breath and squeezed her anger out through the button on the side of the radio. "Just get the sheriff here. I'm not looking for a judge and jury. I'm looking for an officer of the law. Perhaps you're in the wrong business, *Billy*."

She threw the radio down, fuming as she wore a path back and forth stem to stern. Her camera swung with each turn, and she remembered it had taken a beating against the metal wheel. She pulled the camera strap over her head to inspect the machine. All looked good. No cracks or damage on the outside. The power went on with no problem and a sense of relief spread threw her. The last pictures of the swooping hawk appeared on the screen. A majestic creature with power and grace, beauty and… pain came through. Was she looking for her mate? Did she think he left her of his own will? Redtails mated for life. This bird had to be hurting beyond understanding. If only she knew he hadn't left her, but was taken from her by malicious hands.

"We're going to get her, I promise," Rachelle stated up

at the sky. She took a deep breath to calm her nerves and flipped to the next picture.

The photo of Gage and her on the ledge appeared. The roaring ocean and the rock she ridiculously thought was shaped like a heart protruded up behind them. Rachelle zeroed in on her face where her eyes closed in the moment Gage draped his arms around her and pulled her close. He'd surprised her, and she'd latched on to his forearm, never wanting to let go. And he...

Rachelle paused at the look sweeping across Gage's face. His eyes were pressed tight, too, but tears seeped out of their corners. He looked as pained as the hawk missing her mate did.

Was that what this was? Gage knowing he would be leaving her behind? If he felt this way, why couldn't he stay? What could be more important than their love? What could keep him from staying?

Gage said he needed to leave because of Marcus and the danger the warlord would bring to her shores, but if the man was caught, then she and Gage would be free to love. Wouldn't they?

Unless Gage wanted to leave for a different reason?

The treasures. Did he care more about finding them than her? Was that the real reason they couldn't be together? Gold and silver were the real treasure of his heart? She supposed she couldn't blame him. She didn't feel much like a treasure. But she still loved him, even if he didn't feel the same way.

Rachelle studied Gage in the picture. His face expressed love. She was certain of it. Maybe he just didn't know that's what it was. He grew up an orphan. Maybe he didn't understand love. Maybe the man was just confused. He was like the writer of the Proverbs verse from the cavern wall. Gage was amazed by his feelings for her, but he also didn't understand them. He didn't understand they were a part of each other now. Their courses were forever changed, and their hearts forever belonged to the other.

She just had to show him. Prove it to him in the best way possible. By helping him get back the only home he ever had.

With the decision made, Rachelle pushed the code to the gun drawer. It clicked, giving her access. The black revolver waited for her hand to curl around its mahogany handle. It would give her a fighting chance if she had to go up against Jolene's submachine guns.

But could she really shoot it at Jolene? At anyone or anything?

Rachelle thought of the hawk. Instantly, the deep-rooted anger inside her bubbled up like hot lava. That vicious beast of a storm in her said *yes*.

Rachelle replaced her camera in the gun drawer and slammed the door before she wavered in her decision.

"What do you plan on doing with that?" A voice from behind whipped her around.

Jolene stood with her hands holding her Uzi, not a trace of fear showing in her face or stance.

"I'm going to make sure justice is done." Rachelle raised the gun. It shook in her hand, but she held it there. She locked her legs to hold her in the rocking boat. "You've tried to kill me multiple times. You killed the hawk. You need to be stopped before you hurt someone else."

"Like who? Gage? If I was going to kill him, I would have done it under the sea, and I'd be long gone by now. As he will be shortly. He got what he wanted. His boat. You'll never see him again. Now either shoot the gun or drop it before I shoot mine."

Rachelle raised it higher, her hold steadying with each breath, but still she kept her finger off the trigger.

"That's what I thought." Jolene smirked and stepped over the railing into the boat. "You probably can't kill your own lobsters."

"Stop right there, or I will shoot you. I mean it! You don't know anything about me. You don't know what I'm capable of. I have it in me and will pull this trigger. Especially if it means keeping you from hurting Gage."

Jolene's gaze left the gun to look out to sea. "Just like I said, he doesn't need your help because he's leaving. See for yourself." Jolene nodded to a place past Rachelle's shoulder.

"I'm not falling for that." Rachelle kept the gun raised and eyes on Jolene.

"Doesn't change the fact that the *Getaway* is getting away. You may not fall for my words, but you did fall for the bad guy. Wasn't your father a bad guy? That's gotta kill to know you fell for someone just like him."

Rachelle's lips quivered, but she wouldn't let Jolene get to her.

Then a boat's horn blared behind her.

Rachelle whipped around to see the *Getaway* leaving the inlet and heading out to sea. The lofty waves smashed against its hull as though they tried to stop the yacht from making its escape.

Gage was leaving just as Jolene said. Leaving without saying goodbye. Leaving her behind.

That's why he cried in the photo. He knew as soon as he found his boat he'd be gone. It was probably guilt that made him cry.

Not love.

But was Jolene right? Had she really fallen for someone like her father? Was Gage a killer?

In the next second, the gun in her hand went flying overboard as Jolene knocked it with the most powerful punch Rachelle had ever felt. Before she could react, she felt an even more powerful punch upside her head. One that sent her reeling backward into the wheel of her boat.

Pain wrenched though her back, but she went at Jolene with her head down and knees locked, making contact with her legs. She plowed into the woman, sending them both flying over the low railing and into the low tide.

Rachelle tried to stand, but Jolene grabbed a chunk of hair in her fist and twisted. Bright lights of pain burst in Rachelle's head and brought her back to her knees. Her arms reached out to make contact, missing flesh by mere inches.

There was no way Jolene would let her go alive. And Gage wouldn't be coming to shield her this time. Billy Baker probably hadn't told Sheriff Matthews yet, and even if he had, he wouldn't make it in time to save her.

It was kill or be killed, and that was all there was to it.

But how could she get the upper hand with a woman who made killing a sport? With a woman triple her strength? It wouldn't be a match of strength but a match of wills.

Jolene dragged Rachelle out onto the rocky shore. Her knees bore the brunt of the pain on the sharp stones and crippled her more. Her yell resonated with each piercing cut, but Jolene pulled her along without a care. Nausea filled Rachelle's belly. She swallowed it down with a determination to stand to her feet. She had to fight back. Now.

Rachelle pushed up to one foot. It was all she could get under her, but it would have to do. She used the strength in that one leg to rear up to her full height, which still didn't give her an even playing field, but her quick agility was all she needed to catch Jolene off guard. The woman hadn't been expecting the flat of Rachelle's palm to come into such an abrupt and forceful blow at her midsection.

Jolene went sprawling flat on her back. Shock swathed her face at first and then red rage took it over. "You're dead," she said, and came to her feet before Rachelle could prepare to fight or take flight. Jolene raised the long black gun strapped around her and aimed it at Rachelle. One flick of her finger and life would be over. Rachelle had nowhere to run.

"I'll take you to the treasure." The words spilled from Rachelle's mouth just before Jolene's trigger finger cut her life off forever.

"You know where it is?"

Rachelle nodded a few times, but said in a low mumble, "I have an idea."

"Meaning you don't." Jolene left spittle on Rachelle's face as she leaned in, pointing the barrel into Rachelle's chest.

Rachelle stood still, not daring to move. "I have a clue that will lead us there. Gage didn't even know about it. You'll be one step ahead of him."

Jolene smirked. "I like that." She swiped dripping water from her chin. "Fine, I won't kill you, yet. You've bought yourself a few hours to prove your usefulness, but that's it. Let's go."

Jolene let her gun fall at her chest and grabbed Rachelle's upper arm, yanking her toward the path that led up the back of the cliff.

"Where are we going?"

"To my hideout," Jolene said with a shove to Rachelle's back.

One last look over her shoulder, and Rachelle saw the sails of Gage's yacht billowing in the whipping wind, the stern of his boat with the word *Getaway* scrawled across it. His black flag with Psalm 18:16 flapping at the top of its masthead.

*He reached down from heaven and recued me. He drew
me out of deep waters.*

The words echoed through her head as she sent a silent
prayer up to God. *Lord, help me. I need to be rescued, too.
I may not be a treasure, and not worth Your time, but my
mom is, and she needs me. For her, Lord. Will You rescue me for her?*

The waves crashed behind her in answer. Jolene led her
up and up to an unknown destination, then pushed her off
the path and into the woods a ways before they came to a
clump of rocks with thick branches covering them.

"What is this?" Rachelle asked.

Jolene tore away the thatch of twigs, exposing a dark
opening. "Your home for the next few hours. Now get in
there."

The small opening led into a long thin cave, much like
the others on the other side of the island. "I had no idea
there was another cave over here," she said as they came to
a wider clearing. She mumbled, "I hate these caves. They
give me the creeps."

"Yes, I seem to remember you saying that last time we
met in one," Jolene said, and picked up a bright orange
rope. Did she plan to tie her up? "This time you won't have
Gage or anyone to help you out."

On one end of the rope, Jolene worked to create a bowline knot with a single loop. Before Rachelle could figure out what Jolene planned, the woman brought the loop
down over Rachelle, yanking it tight. "Get in."

"Get in? Get in where?"

"There." She pointed to a darkened surface about ten
feet away. Only it wasn't a surface. It was the lack of one.

A hole. A dark cavernous hole.

Rachelle's hope of escaping diminished in the same
way the light did as the hole went deeper. "You want me

to climb down the hole? I don't know how to scale rocks." Her words from earlier with Gage came flooding back.

"You're not scaling. You're rappelling."

"I don't know how to do that, either." Her voice cracked in panic. She'd never get away now.

"Then you're going to fall and get a boo-boo. Either way, you're going in. Now move, or I'll throw you down, and I'm pretty sure that'll be worse."

"Why do I need to go down there at all?"

"I need to go make your boat disappear and can't have you making a run for it. Plus, if you decide to start yelling, no one will hear you from down there. Now move. And I won't ask again."

Rachelle's hands shook as she tightened the ropes around her. Jolene knew her knots well. She took her first step toward the pit. Questions ran through her head. What if the rope didn't hold, or what if it was too long? What if it was too short? What if Jolene let go of the lead?

Rachelle figured she should plan on the last one and not depend on Jolene playing fair.

Rachelle bent down and sat with her legs dangling over the edge. "You're not going to get away with this? All you're doing is racking up the crimes you're going to have to pay for."

"Just add them to the list of my many other outstanding warrants all over the world. I haven't been caught yet. I'm not worried. I have quite a happy life."

Rachelle clamped down on her teeth as the fire in her roared to life. "Spoken like a true selfish person. Don't you get it? Somebody has to pay for your happiness. Do you ever think of the people you've left in your wake? People left to pick up the pieces from your crimes. People who have lost the loved ones you killed."

"It comes with the life we live. I'm surprised Gage

didn't tell you how it was. Killing comes with the territory."

"Gage didn't kill anyone."

Jolene barked with laughter. "I knew you were young, but I honestly didn't think you were naive. Honey, Gage is no better than me. Trust me, he's killed before. There's a reason why he's now the captain of the *Getaway*. I gotta give him credit. It took him a while to overtake Pete, but when the opportunity presented itself, he took it. I always thought Marcus was wrong about Gage. He never thought Gage had what it took to be part of our band, but as it turns out, he did."

"What it takes? You say that like it's something to be proud of. What happened to you that made you think life isn't precious? Every life has value and should be protected and respected."

"Blah-blah. I'm tired of listening to you. Get in the hole before you end up with my boot treads on your back."

Rachelle took a deep breath and held it as she turned her body and lowered herself down to find footing for the fronts of her feet to rest on. Her trembling hands searched out sharp curves and indents in the rock that would make temporary handles for them.

"Even you, Jolene," Rachelle said as she lowered her body down below the surface. Right before the pirate disappeared above, Rachelle said, "You're valuable, too."

"Spare me." The woman came to the edge and looked down. "You're only saying that because you're down there and I'm up here. If this was the other way around, you would be back to your vengeance crusade, demanding my head on a picket."

Rachelle's foot slipped from its foothold. She grabbed tight to the rocks while her foot dangled and searched blindly for safety. She found it and leaned her sweating forehead against the cool rock. She exhaled and inhaled slow deep breaths before she took the next step down.

Darkness enveloped her even more with each level downward. Fear plagued her with questions of what she would find down at the bottom. Then her foot hit bottom, and it was time to find out.

At first, she could do nothing but hold tight to the rocks and press against them. As soon as she stepped back the truth would be revealed. Rats came to mind. And bugs. Lots of bugs.

"You still alive?" Jolene called from above, a little too much joy threading her words.

"Yes, sorry to disappoint you, but I made it safely."

"Don't get too smug. I might forget you're down there. Now untie the rope. It's going bye-bye. I'll send it back down when you can be of some use to me. *If* that ever happens."

If? Rachelle's small victory of surviving the drop plummeted as she began to untie the knots, her fingers trembling and making slow work.

"Hurry up!"

"I'm going as fast as I can. It's dark down here. I can't see what I'm doing. Can you shine some light down here?"

Rachelle stepped back, a hissing sound followed her movement.

She jerked and swung around. A hissing sound. That could only mean one thing. "Jolene! There are snakes in here!"

"Yeah, I know. I put them in there." Jolene's laughter echoed down from above. "You want to change all that gibberish you were just spewing about even *me* being valuable? You should have shot me when you had the chance."

Rage flared up in Rachelle. "You're right. I should have." Without thinking, she yanked the rope with both hands. Jolene let out a shriek as she fell to the edge of the hole. But she released it and the rope drifted down and landed with a thud. Snakes hissed and slithered.

"Hey!" Jolene yelled down from where Rachelle had pulled to the edge of the hole. "Send that back up here!"

"Come down and get it."

"Oh, I will, and when I do, you're dead. You won't get another opportunity to do me in, I can promise you that. Now, I'm off to go hide your boat. No one will ever find you again."

Jolene disappeared from view, and Rachelle called out, "Jolene! You can't leave me in here!" When no answer came after multiple shouts, Rachelle knew it was no use. She also knew she couldn't stay here. But the only way out was up again.

Slowly, she found the rope and pulled it close, winding it up until the last foot of its length found her hand.

The snakes hissed, and Rachelle sidestepped away from the sound. They could sense her, but she could not see them. A few steps and her feet met a large rock. She reached out to feel the outline and realized it was a few feet off the ground and might give some leverage. Dropping the rope on top, she pulled herself up on it.

With the snakes below and unable to touch her, she already felt safer. But not safe enough to hang around. She leaned back against the wall and gazed up to the dim light at the opening and breathed deep as she planned her next move. A ledge off to her right caught her attention.

With careful balance, Rachelle stood on the boulder and made a grab for the part that protruded out. Ten tries with no contact had her breathing heavy and no closer to escape.

I have to get out of here before Jolene comes back. She'll never let me go alive.

Rachelle hunched down and felt for the rope on the rock

at her feet. Her fingers found the braided cord, but she hesitated to make a full grasp at first. A visual of one of the snakes came to mind and made her think of the Proverbs verse. *A serpent on a rock.* When she was certain she only held the rope and not a serpent, she worked from feel and memory to knot the rope in a bowline loop. She would hopefully be able to swing it up on the jutted out piece of ledge and lasso it on. After that point she should be able to climb up and out.

But first to make that connection with ledge and loop.

And hope it didn't come loose, sending her down into the snake pit.

A shiver ran up her spine before she refocused on her task.

I can do this. And then I'm going to go find that sunken ship.

The Proverbs verse mentioned serpents on a rock as one of the clues. If the person who carved the verse into the wall meant for the verse to lead the way to the ship, then the treasure couldn't be far from here.

She would find it, but she didn't plan on telling Jolene, or Gage, that she found it. That was, of course, *if* she ever saw him again. At the moment, she hoped she never did. He knew how she felt about people making choices that left others to pay for the consequences.

Rachelle stood and made a toss for the ledge with her loop.

It fell to the floor in a den of hisses.

How many are down there? She pulled the rope back for another try and tried not to think about the snakes, promising herself Gage would pay for this.

He had brought danger to her home all for a treasure that didn't belong to him. He came on a boat that didn't belong to him. The man it did belong to had to pay with is life so Gage could claim it. Now, here she was stuck down in a hole having to scale a rock wall all because Gage wanted his treasure. He didn't care who had to pay for his deeds or who he left in his wake when he set sail.

At least he would set sail without the treasure. She took gratification in this fact, and with more determination than ever, she swung her rope onto the ledge…and it held tight. A strong tug told her it would hold her up, too.

She took her first step back up the wall, arms shaking at first with the exertion as the rope guided her up. She focused on the ledge above, and after a few more steps, she was able to curl her fingers around the ledge.

Tremors assaulted her muscles. A guttural sound escaped her lips as her elbows took the brunt of hoisting the rest of her body up and onto the ledge.

She'd made it.

Or, at least halfway. The distance left offered no more ledges to loop.

She was on her own with finding hand and footholds.

She felt for footholds first. The higher the better. Her foot found a secure place about two feet up, but she also needed a handhold before she made the climb.

Her hands felt high above her until they found a protrusion good enough. She held tight and lifted her body up. With her free hand she reached up and felt the top of the hole.

She was almost there! Now to find another foothold so she didn't fall all the way back down.

No, I won't think like that. Just keep going.

"The sheriff's out at your boat, so I'll have to move it later," Jolene's voice carried from above.

The pirate was coming back!

Rachelle couldn't waste another second looking for the

best foothold. Anyone would have to do. She couldn't be caught like this. Jolene would kick her down for sure.

Rachelle reached up with, first, one hand then the other. Her head resurfaced from the pit of darkness next. She could have shouted for joy, but there was no time for that. She used every last ounce of strength to lift her body up and down flat on the floor.

Her breaths came fast and hard, but there could be no time for rest. She crawled out on her elbows away from the hole and pulled the rope up her back and over her head to free her body from it completely. She crawled behind a rock as a voice called from the passageway, "How did you get out?"

Jolene stood in the clearing.

She came running up behind the rock with extended arms and hands like claws. They latched onto Rachelle's hair and pulled her up onto the rock. "Now you're going down the fast way."

Rachelle twisted and turned in the opposite direction. She pushed her muscles to their capacity, knowing if Jolene threw her down the hole, she'd never come back up.

Rachelle pulled back and swung her legs out, catching Jolene on the backs of her knees. The woman crumpled to the floor but shot right back up again. Rachelle bent her knees and sprung them out as though they were a coil. They found their mark right at the gun on Jolene's chest.

Air whooshed out of Jolene's lungs, and Rachelle bent her legs to kick out again before the woman found her breath. Jolene went sprawling back, her arms flapping in circles, and then she disappeared over the edge of the hole with a single screech.

Rachelle sat frozen on the rock. Fear and shock stunned her into a paralyzing silence.

She'd just killed Jolene. In a split second, she'd killed someone.

Guilt consumed her, leaving her breathless and aching with a pain that increased with each passing second. Her lungs screamed as her heart broke. Her mind fragmented to a million *if only*'s.

If only she didn't have this anger in her. If only she was better than her father. But at least she had her answer once and for all. The killer inside her had won.

Rachelle placed a trembling hand over her mouth and closed her eyes.

"Help me," a whimper of a voice called up from the hole. "I can't hold on. Help me."

Jolene was alive.

Rachelle jumped to her feet and ran to the edge. She couldn't see where Jolene was, but judging by the sound of her voice she was about halfway down.

Rachelle didn't think twice. She scooped up the rope and tied the end around the rock. She knew she had to help the woman to safety, but she also knew once Jolene resurfaced, the perilous fight would return. Rachelle wouldn't count on the pirate being remorseful. But Rachelle would never live with herself if she walked away without helping Jolene to survive.

She threw the rope down in the direction Jolene hung. "You are valuable, Jolene. Whether you want to believe it or not, you are valuable."

Then she ran as fast as she could back through the tunnel, bursting through the brush and twigs at the opening. She pushed her feet at a breakneck speed to get down the path and to the shore.

Her boat sat in the same place she'd left it, but no other boats were around. If Sheriff Matthews had been here, he was gone now. Rachelle cleared the railing and ran up to the wheel. Her keys were still in the ignition. She gave the engine fuel and pulled up anchor. Her head stayed locked on the path, waiting for Jolene to come barreling down after her with her gun strapped to her. Rachelle pushed the throttle to full speed ahead and promised herself a faster boat after this. It wasn't until she passed the rock shaped like a heart that she took her first breath.

She also took in the black clouds overhead. The storm hovered above, whipping water with its gusts of wind. She needed to get home before the clouds opened up, or she would jump from one boiling pot of danger into another.

Rachelle turned the wheel to her right to make the curve around the island, but a speck of something white against the black clouds caught her attention.

Sails.

Gage's sails.

He should be long gone by now. What had stopped him? The storm? It couldn't be his conscience, she thought skeptically.

Rachelle turned the wheel to find out. She had a few words to say to the criminal that not even the storm would stop her from saying.

Water sloshed up over her railings, pouring onto her deck. Her two hands gripped the helm steady through the choppy waves. Her mind split its focus between her destination and arriving there safely. Gage spoke about her vengeance being her victory. She wanted to make sure he saw her victory firsthand.

And dying before she arrived wouldn't do.

The yacht grew in size as she neared, but a small boat tied to its stern also became clear in the surf. A green sheriff department's boat bobbed along beside it. Apparently, it wasn't Gage's conscience that stopped him, but the law. When Deputy Baker said he'd come and investigate, she'd been angry about his accusations against Gage. Now she took satisfaction in the fact that vengeance and justice would be done today. She'd show Gage how she stood back up on her feet, then she'd let the deputy cuff him and take him away.

THIRTEEN

A cold, hard floor pressed into Gage's right cheek. His hands wouldn't work to push his body up, and his eyes felt laden down as though a pair of his diver's weighted belt bags covered them. A wet, sticky substance pooled by his mouth. Saliva? He pushed his tongue out for a slow lap to find the unmistakable metallic taste of blood. Jolene had beat him up badly and left him for dead.

But where?

He focused on opening his eyes again, but it was no use. Were they swollen shut? Was that why they wouldn't work? Were his hands broken, too?

Gage gritted his teeth through the pain of making his fingers move. When he managed to bend them and then spread them a few times, a flicker of hope surged through him. His hands worked.

And so did his ears.

The sound of engines roared around him and vibrated against his face. Were they his boat's engines he could hear? Did that mean he was still on his boat? If not his, he was on someone's, for sure. The rocking sways nearly sent him slipping and sliding across the floor. He tried to sense if the boat moved through the water and had to believe it did. But for how long? Were they hours out to sea?

Hours from Stepping Stones…and Rachelle?
Rachelle.

Gage groaned with pain in every muscle and joint. He had to stop the boat and get back to her. Although, if Jolene commandeered the boat, then Rachelle was safe.

Except every ache and pain said this assault had been carried out by another. A much stronger, vicious man with a vendetta as wide as the sea.

Marcus had arrived and found him.

It had to be the pirate boss who'd knocked him out and roughed him up. Jolene was a strong woman, but hand to hand combat wasn't her MO. She would have knocked him out and tied him up to bring him to her boss, but this brutality spoke of retaliation. Jolene didn't have a score to settle with him. Only Marcus did.

But if Jolene had stayed behind on Stepping Stones, Rachelle would be in for the fight of her life. A fight for her life.

Gage pushed up on his elbows and lifted his chin to look out from below the swollen slits of his eyes. His jaw ached from the pressure of his locked teeth. He breathed deep and raised his body to his knees. The boat rocked hard to his right and sent him flying back.

"Aw!" he yelled from the pain. The bright florescent lights above blinded him and tortured his throbbing head. But the light also meant his eyes were open enough to see it.

He waited for the dizziness to abate, then rocked his body to his left side and back onto his stomach. Again, he made the push to his elbows, then knees. The boat swayed beneath him. Were they moving? It had to be stopped. For good. The only way to shut the boat down permanently was to disable the engines. And not just disable them, but sabotage them so no one could restart them ever again.

Marcus would never believe the captain of the beautiful *Getaway* would damage his own boat. Probably why the warlord had thrown him in here in the first place. And Gage was certain Marcus threw him, maybe even twice.

Gage reached for a wall bar to steady him as he stood on shaky legs. After stabilizing his body to the motion and his injuries, he took the few steps to his pretty 3516 engines. He rubbed a gentle hand across their pristine, white and chrome exterior. "Sorry, darlings, but it has to be done. You and I won't be traveling the world any longer, but you did good. And trust me, it's for a worthy cause."

Gage took steady steps to the tool drawer for a ratchet, a socket set and two screwdrivers, then made his way back to the engine control modules. The little ten-by-eight black boxes were the brains to the engine. A few cranks of the pin connectors broke the EMCs apart, bringing the throb of the generator to a screeching and groaning halt.

Silence.

Gage listened for any sounds above. Would Marcus come barging down the stairs with murder in his eyes? It would be any second now if he did.

Gage took a screwdriver to the bilges. He couldn't delay if he was to stop Marcus permanently. A pulled drain plug and the oil pan drained. The coolant had to go, too.

And with that, the *Getaway* wouldn't be going anywhere anytime soon. She still had her sails, but her days of crisscrossing the ocean at high speed were over. The engine's fluids poured out with goodbye tears, and Gage gave her chrome finish one more pat.

He expected the disappointment to cut him down worse than Marcus's hands had, but a vision of Rachelle needing his help usurped his pain. He'd deal with his life after hers was preserved. Rachelle's came first. He had to get to her before she lost it forever. Would he be too late to prove to her that her life had value? He meant what he said to his engines. It was for a worthy cause. A very worthy cause.

Lead me, Lord, and if I'm too late, show her Your love. Rescue her like You rescued me. She'll think it's for someone else, because she doesn't know the way You see her. Show her how bright and beautiful You see her. How she is worth more to You than any lost coin.

The exit was locked, so Gage grabbed a crowbar and popped the lock on the door. The door fell ajar for him to peer out. He had no intention of going above deck. His small launch boat would take him back to Stepping Stones. He'd get help and come back for Marcus, once and for all, but only after Rachelle was safe.

Two steps toward the launch door and a man's voice boomed above. The floors between them muffled it, but it was definitely a man's. Then another man spoke. There were two of them. Marcus came with reinforcements. How many more were up there?

Gage limped on. There wasn't time to find out. Another shout came from outside. Only this time a woman's voice could be heard, and it didn't sound like Jolene's deep voice. It held a sweet tinkling sound even in the harsh words she spoke.

Rachelle? Could it be? He would recognize her angry voice anywhere, and judging by the words coming out of her now, she wanted someone to hang.

Him?

Gage couldn't figure it out. Not now. All he knew was she could not board this boat. He had to stop her, even if that meant he ran blindly above deck. He faced the stairs, the launch forgotten.

At the first tread, one of the men spoke, and Gage recognized the voice as belonging to Sheriff Matthews. The law enforcer's voice rushed like a welcoming wave over

Gage. Help had arrived. Owen and Special Agent Caden and whoever else Owen brought with him would take down Marcus for good. Gage would even welcome Baker aboard.

But why was Rachelle the only one shouting? Her voice carried down from the salon. She'd boarded. Gage took the first steps up, but then everything went quiet. Too quiet. What was going on?

He stepped up two more treads, then heard Sheriff Matthews bellow, "Rachelle! Watch out!"

Gage pushed his battered body past its limits and up the stairs as fast it would go. At the door, he burst through and stopped in the middle of his salon when something went flying past his face. He feinted back, his arms went up in a reflex, and his gaze shot to the object that nearly went through his head.

A knife stuck out from his wooden walls, its black handle still vibrating from the impact. Gage couldn't take his eyes off it. All he could wonder was who had thrown it.

He scanned the salon and froze at a certain, notable tattoo inked on the back of a man's bald head. The sight quickly confirmed Gage's suspicions about who stuffed him in the engine room.

A black letter *P* with a sword cut through it—Marcus's signature stamp. This could only mean Marcus had officially arrived, and he was the knife wielder.

But who had been his target?

A sick feeling spread through Gage as his mind wrestled with the possibility that it could have been Rachelle. He denied it, even when he noticed her lying flat on the floor.

Rachelle sprawled on the floor face-first. Owen had shoved her so hard and fast, and she still wasn't totally sure why. He'd wanted her to get back in her boat, but she refused. Not until she'd seen Gage.

But Owen had been relentless. He whispered something about a phone call from the feds today. He said, "Things are not what they seem."

She sat up and flipped around, resting on her hands. "What was that—" Her words clogged her throat as a lump of confusion bulged up. Owen sat also on the floor, but the way he slumped in silence against the wall told her he wasn't getting back up.

Rachelle's gaze pinged around the close quarters. Two men remained standing, but Gage grabbed her full attention. His face was swollen and his lip bled from the corner. Her mouth fell open in silence. Every sharp word she'd planned to say to him washed away like the color in his skin. He was as pale as a landlubber at sea.

"Gage?" she said with uncertainty in her voice. "What happened? What's going on?"

"Can't you just go away and leave me alone? Get off my boat. Now." Gage's eyes stormed up like the black clouds outside. His words were daggers flying her way. Each one cut her deep to the core. She took a few crab walk steps backward away from the whole confusing and turbulent atmosphere. His sickened expression matched the swirls in her stomach, and she didn't know which was worse. The storm outside? Or the one in here?

Gage turned his face away. At first he looked at something on the wall and then to Special Agent Caden. His stance straightened to his full height like some kind of Mr. Tough Guy. Was he showing off for the federal agent? Or did he plan to try to kill him, too?

"Did you knock Owen out?" she screeched in shock, then brought her voice under control. "Why would you hurt him? Did he find out you killed before? Agent Caden, arrest him. He's a killer. He killed Pete Masters."

Agent Caden crossed his arms. "No, he didn't. I did."

Rachelle froze. "I…I don't understand."

Gage turned saddened eyes on her. The stormy blue daggers evaporated, leaving behind a misty sorrow. "This isn't Special Agent Caden, Rachelle." His lips curved down as his shoulders also drooped. "This is Marcus."

"Marcus?" Rachelle mumbled, and looked at a smiling Special Agent Caden, who wasn't Special Agent Caden, but *Marcus?* As in the pirate boss *Marcus?*

"Show her your tattoo, Marcus. The one you hid under your hat the whole time you paraded around town pretending to be something you're not."

Special Agent Caden turned his head just enough for her to see the black *P*. Her mind caught up. Rachelle sucked air into her lungs, and she peeled her eyes away to look to Gage for an explanation. His jaw ticked, and his fists clenched, but he'd yet to look her way. "It's really true?" she asked. The fact that Marcus showed it freely only meant one thing: They weren't going to live to tell anyone about it.

Marcus answered. "It's true." Also freely and willingly. Not good. "And nice try, Gage, trying to protect Rachelle with making her think you didn't care about her by telling her to get off your boat. But, I've seen you enough times around town to know you like having her around, so sorry, I'm not buying what you're selling. You care a great deal for her, and that will come in handy. But, I will say, that was very admirable what you just did there. Saving her by rejection." His hand went to his chest. "Oh, how my heart aches at your selflessness. I think I might shed a tear." His smile dropped. "Not really."

"How did you do it, Marcus?" Gage asked. "Did you kill the real agent sent here to help?"

Marcus smiled again. A real, jolly smile that sickened

Rachelle's stomach. She exhaled with a whimper at what this all meant.

The pirate boss had been on her shores practically the whole time. He knew everything about her. There would be no hiding anything. There would be no escaping a man who infiltrated the criminal law enforcement process with such ease.

Her gaze drifted to Owen. Her heart ached for her friend. For Miriam and their son. She was afraid to ask, but had to know. "Did you kill Owen, too?"

"Another admirable act," Marcus said. "Sheriff Matthews saved your life when he pushed you to the floor. But don't worry, he's just out cold." Marcus walked over to the wall and reached up.

Rachelle saw the knife handle before he yanked it from the wall in the exact location she had been standing in when she entered the salon. Owen had told her to leave, that things were not as they seemed.

"He knew," she said, and looked up at Marcus. "Owen knew you were a fake. He tried to tell me."

"Yes, he figured it out," Marcus said and turned to Gage. "But only because Gage's maps were wrong. The ship's not where you marked it, Gage. Some treasure hunter you are. If I'd found it sooner, I would have been long gone before Matthews got the call from the real Caden's supervisor." Marcus strolled up to Rachelle, the knife curved out in his hand. He brought the sharp tip to her cheek and glided it down to her chin with a sigh. "You are beautiful in a dark, exotic way. Those eyes are amazing. They flash as bright as Colombian emeralds." He swiped the knife again. "Such a shame."

"Don't touch her," Gage said. He raced up behind her and yanked her back by her shoulders. "You don't want her. You want me, and now you have me. It's all over.

I'm done running. You win. The *Getaway* is yours. Let Rachelle go back in her boat, and we can go. You can kill me at sea and throw me overboard."

"No!" Rachelle grabbed Gage's hands at her shoulders as she thought through her next words. They'd worked with Jolene, maybe they would work with Marcus. "You don't just want Gage and the *Getaway*. You also want the treasure. What kind of pirate would you be if you left it behind?"

"And I'm supposed to believe you know where it is?" Marcus laughed. "The two of you are made for each other. Both of you are selling things I'm not buying." He brought the knife close to her face again.

Rachelle held still as she spoke.
"There be three things which are
too wonderful for me,
Yea, four that I know not:
The way of an eagle in the air,
the way of a serpent upon a rock,
the way of a ship in the midst of the sea…"

She swallowed deep, the gulp heard by all. "And the way of a man with a maid."

"What is that supposed to be?"

"That's the clue to finding the treasure." She let her eyes drift in the direction of the place the *Maria's Joy* rested. Deep in her heart, she knew that's where the sunken ship lay. "It wasn't the pirates who sank her. Pirates wouldn't do that. It was the one person who didn't want the *Maria's Joy* to fall into their hands and be spoiled and destroyed by their criminal deeds. They would use her as a pirate ship, attack and pillage more ships with her. Unless he stopped them."

"Who?" Marcus asked,

"The clergyman. Every ship had one on board, especially coming out of Spain. They must have kept him as a prisoner. I'd be willing to say he gave his life bringing her down by crashing her into the rocks. But first, he left his clue. A scripture from the Book of Proverbs carved into the wall of a dark cavern. Then, he took her out and gave her peace."

"How sweet, but all I care about is where the ship is now. And you're going to show me." Marcus reached out and snatched her upper arm. He yanked her to her feet and dragged her to the table with the map. "Find it," he said, tossing her down on the bench seat, keeping the knife at her throat. "Gage, won't you sit down at my table." The invitation was expressed more as a command.

Gage stood for thirty seconds before he gave in and sat across from her. He implored her with his blue eyes while his hand rested on the tabletop. His fingers splayed out as though he reached for her. She dropped her own hand to the table and did the same. The corners of his lips curved in a sad smile. She wanted to tell him it was all right. She knew he could do nothing to help her with a knife aimed at her neck.

"You have to let her go if she tells you." Gage raised angry eyes to Marcus.

"Sure," he replied quickly, but why should she believe him? Gage's frown told her he didn't, either.

"Emerald Point is the place the clergyman spoke of. The birds of prey and snakes live abundantly here." Rachelle pointed to the cliffs on the map. "But it's when he says a ship in the midst of the sea that he's telling us where he put her out to sea. He tells us with the last line of the scripture." Rachelle lifted her eyes to Gage. Pain and anger ripped across his eyes. He felt useless to her, unable to save her.

She was about to be destroyed forever, and he could do nothing about it. She needed to tell him she didn't blame him. She'd had enough with casting blame. It served no purpose and only killed relationships and kept people hidden. "He tells us when he writes how the way of a man with a young woman amazes him. It's love that brings peace. The way of a man with a young woman is how he loves her. He holds her in his heart forever. His heart belongs to her, and hers belongs to him."

"Enough with the riddles. Point to the spot now!"

Rachelle jumped and pointed to the space on the map where the heart rock protruded out from the sea. The next second, Marcus sent his blade flying, point down on the spot. She whipped her hand back just in time from being impaled. Her hand turned cold and shook as she held it near to her chest.

Marcus hooted with laughter. "You're not so tough now. You just wait to see where you're going next. A little birdie told me before I killed him that you don't like to dive."

"You killed the hawk?" Rachelle felt a sickening swirl in her chest.

"Yup, I was already here watching you. I learned quite a bit before I stepped into my role as Special Agent Caden. You may navigate above the water just fine, but below, you're scared to death." Marcus kept his eyes on her as he spoke to Gage. "Get to the helm, Gage. We're going treasure hunting."

The boat tipped to its port side, reminding everyone of the storm barreling in around them.

"Did you not notice? I disabled the engines. We're not going anywhere."

Marcus whipped Rachelle's head back in the same moment he ripped the knife from the table. He brought the knife to rest at her exposed neck and snarled, "You're going to pay dearly for destroying those engines. Until then, open the sails. We're diving."

Gage's face paled even more. His eyes searched hers with remorse while his mouth opened and closed with nothing to stop this mayhem. "You can't dive in this weather," he said. "The sand will be stirred up. It will be a shifting mess, and visibility will be nil."

"Get to the helm, or I'll kill her now."

Gage shook his head and bit down on his teeth but stood and twisted around to head to the wheel.

"Excited, sweetheart?" Marcus asked her.

Rachelle's heart skipped a few beats before she shook her head and swallowed hard.

"There's a first time, and *last* time for everything. Gear up. You're going down. And don't worry if you mess up. You won't be coming back up anyway."

FOURTEEN

Gage tested the weighted square bags in his hands before inserting them into Rachelle's diving belt. "These should allow you to descend and not float. But you need to relax, too. Anxiety will stop you from sinking."

"But I don't want to sink," she mumbled through pale, trembling lips as he snapped her air tank strap in place over her neoprene wet suit. "I don't want to dive at all."

They stood on the dive platform at the stern of the *Getaway,* seconds away from stepping off into a churned-up sea. "I know you don't, and I hate that Marcus is making you, especially under these storm conditions." Gage leaned in and whispered, "But if he plans to kill you, I can help you better down there than up here." He eyed Marcus across the platform pulling on his diving hood. "Stay with me and watch me, okay? Depending on how deep we have to go, we should have a good hour of air in our tanks, but even still, when I give the signal, swim fast. Get to shore before you run out."

"Did you really destroy your engines?"

"Don't worry about it, you just—"

"Why would you do that? The *Getaway* is your home."

"The *Getaway* is mine now," Marcus cut in from behind, obviously picking up on the whispering. Had he heard anything else? "You two are taking way too long to gear up. Enough with the chitchat. Move it."

Gage heard the pirate pull his tank up and over his head to land on his back. The snap of his strap jolted Gage. He fisted his hands at his side instead of in Marcus's face. The best plan for Rachelle's safety was to dive. As long as she could do it safely. "You know she's never dived before," Gage said to Marcus. "I have to give her directions."

"Hurry up." Marcus stepped up beside them. "Those clouds are about to open up real soon."

"You afraid of getting wet?"

"Not at all. I just want to make sure I survive to spend the treasure your little girlfriend is going to find me." He flashed his dive knife at them and made sure they saw him fasten it to his thigh. No words needed for his blaring message.

Gage pressed his lips tight and reaffirmed his plan to get Rachelle far away from Marcus as fast as possible. He didn't want to kill if he could help it, but Rachelle's life came first, and he would do what he had to. Gage reached up and tugged her black diver's hood over her head. Two masks hung from his forearm. He removed hers to place it on her head. "This mask should be your size. Now, what I need for you to do is inhale through your nose and hold your breath as I fit it to your face. Breathe through your mouth only. The mask will suction on and shouldn't leak that way. If it still lets water in, don't panic. It happens. I get water in my mask all the time and sometimes have to adjust it down below."

"Does your mask not fit you?" she asked after her mask covered her nose and eyes.

"I have too many laugh lines. It's hard to make a good suction because of these old crow's-feet. Water leaks in real easy." He tried to flash a reassuring smile, but smiling never hurt so much. And not just because of the swelling from Marcus's fists, but because how could he smile knowing he could be descending Rachelle to her death. "You'd think I'd learn my lesson and stop smiling so much."

"I hope you never stop. Your smile is beautiful and vibrant, and what I noticed first about you…after you stopped moaning from the bends, anyway." Her small smile trembled on her lips.

"Bends. Right." He pointed to the valves on her BC vest. "This here is your buoyancy compensator which contains a bladder that holds gas. These buttons are your vent valve and your dump valve. You'll need to depress these deflation buttons to equalize your air spaces. It fills the bladder with gas and allows you to float slowly up and down. Want to ascend? Push for more gas to be added to your bladder. Want to descend? Let the gas out. But once again, relax and let it take you."

She rubbed her hand over the buttons and closed her eyes in the mask with a nod.

"Good girl, now remember. There can be no breathing inside your mask. That means no breathing through your nose. Keep practicing breathing through your mouth for a few minutes before I put your regulator on."

"She doesn't have a few minutes," Marcus barked beside them.

"You want your treasure or don't you? Let her practice."

Marcus searched the dark sky and out to sea. "Ten seconds."

Rachelle jolted but opened her mouth to practice her new way of breathing.

"Perfect." Gage lifted her next piece of equipment. "Now this is your regulator. You're going to bite down on it as you're breathing through your mouth. I know, it sounds like a lot to remember, but I know you can do it.

You're smart and brave and you will be victorious. Do you hear me, Rachelle? You will be victorious."

Her green eyes widened to half-dollars as her mouth fit around the regulator.

"Remember what I told you about vengeance and victory, right? You will get back on your feet and be victorious. God will lift you out of deep waters and rescue you, just like His word says. Believe it. You are valuable to Him. He is searching for you, and you are more valuable than any coin and any treasure anywhere."

"That's it," Marcus stepped up. "The only thing valuable here is the treasure." He shoved Gage's shoulder, sending him flying back, Marcus's other arm snaked out at Rachelle. One quick push and she went flying backward out over the water.

"Rachelle!" Gage pushed back at Marcus at full force, then yanked on his mask and regulator and jumped out, forcing himself to use the giant stride technique with one leg lifted out and his eyes on the horizon. He really wanted his eyes on Rachelle, but to be sure the water took him in with a clean gulp, he needed this dive to be spot-on.

He sank perfectly and beneath the water, twisting and twisting to find her. Bubbles caught his attention. As he expected, she'd caused a commotion under the water with flailing arms and legs. At this rate, she'd use all her oxygen up before she descended.

Gage swam over to her and grabbed both her upper arms in a vise grip. He squeezed until she calmed enough to notice his face an inch from hers. His headlamp revealed her bulging eyes behind the mask, but he also noticed her regulator bubbled correctly.

Gage took a deep breath of air off his mouthpiece. He then removed it while one of his hands still held on to her. *You're breathing well. Good,* he mouthed with a nod. He beamed a proud smile at her and watched her eyes relax as she, too, realized her success in breathing.

Rachelle's lips curved up around her regulator. She raised her hand to place it on his chest with two taps. Once again the fool woman passed her victory over to someone else.

Gage shook his head and mouthed, *All you. You.* Would she ever understand?

Would she have another day to try?

Gage replaced his regulator as the water above them clouded with Marcus's entry into the water. A scan above showed they'd put a good distance from the surface, and from Marcus. But even so, this was it. This was the moment that Gage's running came to an end. There would be no more flight, but only fight from this moment on. A fight to his death if need be.

But not Rachelle's. Rachelle had to live another day. God still searched for her to claim her as His. Gage wrapped a hand around the back of her neck to pull her forehead to his. She went dark with his headlight blocked, but he took the moment of anonymity to accept his feelings for her. Gage pulled his head back, making sure she could see his face in the light. He pulled his regulator out and mouthed with slow and clear lips, *I...love...you.*

The words came out with ease. They were the truth. He felt his heart stir to life with the realization that Rachelle was his treasure. Not his boat. Not his job. But Rachelle. He watched her face behind her mask. Had she read his declaration with accuracy? Did she understand what she was to him? He may never have another chance to tell her.

The bubbles from her regulator ceased as the look in her eyes dulled. Her typical green emeralds that he'd never been able to say no to averted to his shoulder. The simple turn of her eyes cut him as if they were the sharp gems themselves.

Gage placed his regulator in his mouth. He forced his conscious breath to calm his heart and to ebb the pain in his air-deprived lungs. But after three deep breaths, the ache in his chest remained intact.

So this was what a broken heart felt like.

He'd always dreamed of loving someone, but in his dreams, they loved him back.

Marcus drifted down beside them. He tapped Rachelle on the shoulder with a look behind his mask to say, *Move it.*

She turned her gaze back on Gage, but the dull look he'd seen before had turned to a blazing rage. His confession of love made her angry? She looked ready to kill.

It's kill or be killed. The words she'd spoken before came back to him. She'd told him there was a storm that raged in her. It feared even her. Deep down, in the dark recesses of her soul, was she like her father? A killer waiting to come out?

Were they about the find out?

Rachelle flung her arms wide, and before Gage could stop her, she pressed her BC vent valve and sank deep. Deep, but too fast.

"Rachelle!" he shouted around his regulator. He pressed his own button to try and catch up to her, but every swipe to grasp her ended with an empty hand.

She raced on ahead of him. Worry for her safety kept him dropping. He couldn't lose her.

Gage checked his diver's watch for the depth gauge. He'd dropped a hundred feet already. Anything more than one thirty could be dangerous. Rachelle didn't have a watch and wouldn't know to stop.

Gage continued to drop, keeping his headlight face-down. Her head remained in his sight below him, and he saw her abruptly stop moving. Gage raced on to catch up to her, adding air from his BC to stop beside her on the ocean floor.

He grabbed her arms to face her to him. He took out his regulator and yelled, "Stay with me!" His anger took a backseat instantly, though, to assessing her wellbeing. As far as he could tell she still looked mad. He'd take that as a good sign. He may not like seeing her anger directed at him, but it was better than her showing signs of lethargy or, worse, agony.

He let his arms drift away from her. His hand itched to reach for hers, but he had to be satisfied with knowing she'd survived the descent. Now just to deflect Marcus's attention so she could swim away. Gage stepped out to survey the scene for a possible place for an altercation. His eyes searched through the darkness and the churning sand, but the sand should have been worse. Gage realized they weren't on the ocean floor after all.

They were on the deck of the *Maria's Joy.*

Rachelle stared at Gage's back as he swam around the wrecked ship. He'd told her he loved her. How she wished she could have heard his words, not just read them on his lips. At first, she wondered if she'd read them right. Then she wondered if he meant them. Had they been the parting words of a man about to give his life for her? She knew that's what he planned. Fight Marcus to the death, so she could escape and have her victory. Had he only said he loved her so his death wasn't in vain?

She quickly realized that didn't make sense. Gage was an honest man. He'd come too far in his own victory to blow it all with a final lie.

That's when she got mad. Never had the roar inside her

sounded so loud. The roll of thunder thumped through her chest and up to her head in a cadence that meant war.

War against Marcus. War against the injustice the man of crime had brought to her shores and brought to her and Gage.

But something felt different about this anger in her than all the other times it raged in her. It felt productive instead of destructive. Justified instead of resented. She didn't feel like a victim to another's acts now but rather a warrior ready to fight for goodness.

And both she and Gage would celebrate their win together. She imagined what his profession of love would sound like to her ears when they survived and lifted their bodies out of these waters. She let the desire to hear his words be the determination she needed to outsmart Marcus.

Already she'd beat him down here. Now they just had to find the treasure and use it as bait to trap him, just as the pirate did to Gage with the *Getaway*.

Gage's boat was everything to him. It was his home, and Marcus knew his weakness. He also knew hers was diving. He thought sending her down here would weaken her. And yesterday, it might have.

But not today.

Gage returned to her side, and Rachelle grabbed her regulator to tell him she was with him through this, but he stopped her with a shake to his head.

She needed to tell him she loved him, but what good would she do for him if she drowned herself? She may not feel weakened by being forced to dive, but that was only because she'd stuck to the rules so far.

Well, almost.

She'd left Gage's side when he told her not to. But not again. She reached for his hand and gave it a squeeze. It wasn't a profession of love, but she hoped he read it as her stand to stick by him. His smile around his regulator confirmed her belief in his intelligence.

It also accomplished the same effect it did on land.

How could she get weak in the knees even down under the sea? She didn't know, but instead of overanalyzing, she accepted it as she went with him when he tugged her forward.

So this was Gage's world. To think she'd passed on gaining this glimpse into a part of his life that made him who he was. His excitement at an overturned cannon covered in a greenish conglomerate substance even made her a little giddy. Who'd think old artillery would make the man beam? She couldn't wait to see his reaction when they found the treasure.

A sudden thought dampened her spirits and had her looking above for Marcus. The man still hadn't descended all the way yet. What would he do to them if there wasn't a treasure to be found? What if the clergyman had made off with the coins before he sank the *Maria's Joy?*

Rachelle pushed the thought away. The man of God didn't care about the treasure as much as he cared about the ship. He'd sunk her to save her, not to pocket her wealth. There was no doubt the treasure was down here. She just had to find it. And fast.

Gage led her to the stem of the ship. Or where the stem would have been if the vessel had been intact. The clergyman must have plowed her right into the rock to sink her. Down she came, pouring out her contents. They swam out over the broken part of the ship to find centuries' old debris and sand. He swam down and looked back with a thumbs-up. Apparently, the heap of remains was the golden spot. She'd trust him to know what he was doing.

He lifted piece after piece and let them float down to

the sandy bottom. The water churned up, making viewing impossible. Rachelle reached out for him to tell him to stop but realized he wasn't looking for the treasure. He was trying to cause a sandy chaos to hide her so she could escape.

No, she wanted to tell him, but could only pull him away from the stirred-up sand. They swam back until the water cleared. Another cannon rested below. She drifted down to the ocean floor where her feet landed on a rack of dishes, lying in the sand like dominoes. They were so neatly lined up she wished for an underwater camera to take a picture.

Rachelle smiled around her regulator, especially when she noticed the amount of wildlife swimming by for the first time. Now she really wanted a camera down here.

A school of massive blue marlin swam in her path and kept right on going. The photographs she could capture down here would be amazing. Maybe she could trade in her land camera for an underwater one.

Or trade her landlubber life in for one at sea. The idea didn't seem so far-fetched now.

Sailing would be in her future if she meant to be part of Gage's life crisscrossing the oceans for the next shipwreck. Didn't he already have another wreck to salvage? Down in Peru, if she remembered correctly. Rachelle wondered what kind of fish she could photograph in South America. Probably creatures as bright and vibrant as Gage himself.

She swam a little farther, knowing he followed behind with his head raised to the surface looking for Marcus. His desire to protect her made her feel so cherished. A lifetime experiencing such a feeling would never be enough, but she'd enjoy every day of it.

Sudden images of them cruising out on the open water, dining under the glorious stars, waking to the purple tangerine skies he'd told her about lit her whole body up with a fluttering thrill as she began to believe a life at sea with this enthusiastic and buoyant man was possible.

She turned to look at him, but a right angle shape caught her attention in the sand. Flipping to swim horizontally, she swept away the sand and found the corner of something square. A few more swipes and she exposed another corner. When all four corners lay uncovered, the object sure looked like a chest sunken into the seafloor.

Excitement mushroomed up like the sand around her. She'd made a commotion when she pushed away the sand and couldn't see Gage behind her anymore. She'd promised not to leave his side and she needed to find him. She swam one way but was pulled back hard by her upper arm.

A twist around, she yanked her arm free, expecting to find Marcus. But it was Gage, and he wasn't too happy. Did he think she was leaving him again? She wished she could tell him she'd been about to search for him, not leave his side. She pointed down to the chest, hoping it would make him happy again.

He pointed toward shore.

He still wanted her to swim to shore without him. Marcus had to already be down here somewhere, and Gage knew it. He could be lurking anywhere in the sifting sand, and they wouldn't know it until he was on them. Gage wanted her gone before the pirate caught them by surprise.

But Rachelle believed there could be another way. If this chest contained the gold and silver coins, then they could entice Marcus with the find. Maybe trap him down here somehow. One of these cannons would make a good restraint until the authorities could get down here to detain him.

Gage's life of running could end right now, and she could help him turn the tables on the man who'd spent fifteen years trying to capture Gage, by capturing the man instead.

Talk about vengeance and victory. They would stand back up on their feet together, raise their hands to the sky and thank…

Rachelle paused in her thoughts. *Thank God?* Yes, she nodded. God would lift them out of these deep waters and rescue them. Both of them. Not only Gage, but her, also. God loved her, too. Not because she helped her mom, and not because she wanted to help Gage here today, but because He loved *her*. She was important and valuable in her own right.

Rachelle felt His love now. She also felt God's push to help Gage. Her adrenaline spiked as she dropped to her knees to open the chest. As expected, Gage tugged her arm, but she lifted her head to him and gave him her answer with a heated glare. She wasn't going anywhere, so start helping or face her wrath, and maybe even the wrath of God, too.

No words were needed for him to understand now. He bent down beside her and felt around the chest's edge. His fingers brushed against hers as they searched for the latch. Would it be locked?

Gage ripped away a green, corroded hinge. She didn't think she had to worry about it being locked now. One more rusted-out hinge would be all they needed to open this baby up.

The second came off with ease, and caused Gage's eyes to jump to life. The man made her insides jump to life, too. His love for the hunt was infectious, and together they lifted the lid of the chest up. It was heavy, but the sight inside made her forget the strain on her arms as she held the lid out in front of her to keep it up.

Gold bars lined up neatly in perfect rows. They were

stacked from top to bottom like golden, wrapped candy bars. Their existence shocked her motionless. Gold bars! These things had been down here all this time, and no one had any idea.

Rachelle thought of the three million shipwrecks estimated to be lying on the floor of the oceans. Were they all like this? No wonder Gage lived for the hunt. The find felt like nothing she'd ever experienced. She wanted to keep hunting this burial ground to free more treasure from its hold.

The desire stirred up the realization that she was part of the treasure being freed from its rock-bottom clutches. But like Gage had said, and Rachelle felt the strength in her build as she believed even more, she was the real treasure.

Gage. She had so much to thank him for. She couldn't wait to rise to the surface to tell him. She would wrap her arms around him and glory at being treasured by this man of God.

But first, she would have to free Gage from Marcus's clutches once and for all. Perhaps this lid would make a good restraint if she could remove it and throw it on Marcus. If she could get him lying on his back, his tank would weight him down, too.

Rachelle leaned in, letting the tank on her back push her forward until the lid broke off. The cover dropped in a drift, causing the sand to mushroom up in a cloud. Slowly, the sand diminished, and Marcus floated behind the chest.

Rachelle shrank back, ramming into Gage as Marcus sprang forward, brandishing his knife, the point aimed for the air hose at her shoulder.

Gage's arm reached across her and pulled her to him, but when a cloud of crimson ballooned up in her face, she realized he had taken the slash meant to cut off her air.

Gage's blood filled her vision, paralyzing her. Her air

hose may not have been severed, but her lungs didn't know yet. Air locked in her chest as she watched Gage's blood separate her from Marcus. Slowly, she exhaled at the dispersing mixture of life and sea.

Marcus lunged again, jolting her back to reality, but right before she could push Gage's bleeding hand away, he shoved her back into a fast somersault. Her tank toppled her over with a weight stronger than her muscles to stop the momentum. Three times her body flipped before she could gain control. Her mouth breathing halted and reverted to her land breaths through her nose. The seal of her mask extracted from her face as she lost her focus on the correct breathing technique. Water seeped inside filling halfway as a cold, shaking panic set in. Rachelle pressed it hard to her face, praying for it to stick and stop filling. What if she couldn't see? She wouldn't know how to find Gage. She wouldn't even know up from down.

Slowly, she brought her hands away, waiting to see if the mask would stick tight. Turning her mouth breathing back on, she peered down to the seafloor. Gage fought somewhere in the sandy commotion. Her legs kicked with fervor, and her arms spread wide with cupped hands for paddles. She rushed back to the chest, but both men were gone.

Right to left, Rachelle searched through the murky darkness, her headlight only gave the path in front of her illumination. Everything beyond became part of the mystery of the sea. And Gage was in that murky unknown, bleeding and fighting his life. He would want her to hightail it to the shore. She knew he would, but there could be no victory without him beside her. Rachelle shook her head and made up her mind. There would be no cutting bait today.

Only fishing for pirates.

FIFTEEN

Gage bit down on his regulator to bear the searing pain from his hand while he squeezed Marcus's wrist to force him to drop his weapon. An even playing field needed to be established if he ever wanted to see Rachelle again. Which he did. With a vision of her in orange waders on her fishing boat, her sun-kissed, freckled cheeks shining and green eyes glowing up at him, he sent a quick head butt to Marcus's forehead. Both headlamps smashed to pieces, pitching them into darkness and tripping Marcus up enough to loosen his hold.

Gage felt the blade drift down to the sand at his flippers. He took the opportunity while he could still locate Marcus's mask and yank it loose from his face. Water filled the man's vision, and he struggled with Gage to free Gage's hold. But at the same time, Gage's regulator was ripped out from his mouth. Water filled in as he let go of Marcus to search the darkness around him for his mouthpiece. With each swipe, he prayed Marcus hadn't detached it from the tank.

Pain exploded in his knee. Marcus yanked on his leg, twisting it in unnatural position. Gage elbowed down but only hit the other man's tank. Any second his leg would crack and break, but he couldn't see Marcus to know how to get out of the hold.

And then, a light shown down on Marcus. Gage made out his head and wrapped an arm around his neck to yank him back. The pain in his leg continued, but Marcus looked above at the light coming their way and stilled.

The light. Where was it coming from?

No. It couldn't be. Gage despaired at the realization of whose light illuminated them as he found his regulator floating at the side of his head, still attached to his tank. It just couldn't be. He wanted her to be safe, he thought as he breathed deep, refilling his lungs. He wanted her to be near the shore by now. He wanted her to be climbing the cliffs of Emerald Point in victory.

Not down here paying for his sins.

He ignored his throbbing leg and pushed away from Marcus to find her. High above, he could see her headlamp but not her. Kicking his leg was painful and swimming up didn't seem possible. His hand found the valve to add gas to his bladder and after a few seconds he lifted up to her.

Rachelle scooped her arms around him like a net, and he did the same, but only for a moment. He leaned back, searching her shadowed face under her lamp, and then hugged her again. He should be angry that she hadn't listened, but deep down he didn't want to let her go. He grasped on to her like a lifeline.

She pulled away his hand on her arm and covered it where the blood still leaked out. She pressed hard to stop the flow, but he needed for her not to worry and to go. To get away and save herself.

He pushed hard at her, catching her off guard. Her arms reached out for him, but he hit the vent valve and let it take him down. He watched her as they grew apart. "Go, my love, go!" he said even though she couldn't hear him.

As the distance grew, her lamp caught on something moving around her. *Marcus?* Had he swam up to her? Gage fumbled with his valve to yo-yo himself back up, but his leg jerked back and pulled him down.

He reached down to find Marcus's hand in a death grip. But if Marcus was below him, then who swam above with Rachelle?

Gage searched above as Marcus pulled him farther away from her. Her lamp caught the swimmer in its beam.

"No!" Gage yelled out, sending up a flurry of bubbles from his regulator and jerking his leg from Marcus to no use. Gage sank faster with his eyes peeled above on Rachelle—and the streamlined blue shark circling her. All because she carried *his* blood on her hands.

Rachelle hovered halfway between the seafloor and the water's surface. Her emptying air tank was the least of her worries. A blue shark sniffed around her, the smell of blood in the water an open invitation. She wasn't cut, but the shark didn't know that. He or she was out for a hunt. Rachelle wished that school of blue marlin she'd seen earlier would reappear.

"That's what you really want," she mumbled around her regulator. "I'm not your prey. You don't want me." Rachelle pooled Gage's words to her about sharks and how they'd received a bad rep as vicious human predators. *What had Gage said?* More deaths occurred by vending machines falling on people than by shark attacks.

Rachelle held still in the water and thought she would take the vending machine right about now. Especially when the fish stopped circling her and turned its sleek body to face her. Rows of pointy, razor-sharp teeth glistened in its openmouthed grin as its nose lifted to her.

Slowly, Rachelle reached for her air valve and requested

a few pumps of gas to her bladder. *Come on, fill up, will you?* The gas wouldn't shoot her out of here like a rocket, but every little bit helped. She had to be pushing against the clock and needed the air for her lungs, but if she was killed right here, she wouldn't need the gas anyway.

The shark closed in on her, it's large, black eyes and slender body seemed almost relaxing.

Almost.

Rachelle dared not move a muscle, but then the air in her vest bladder kicked in and buoyed her up just as the shark drifted by below her. Rachelle's flippers nearly skimmed its smooth indigo back.

Would it come back around? Rachelle kicked a few times to propel her farther up while it wasn't looking. The shark stopped again, then swam back to where she'd floated before. It stopped, then in a split second, bent its body nearly in half and jetted below in the direction Gage had dropped.

Gage!

The shark smelled Gage's blood. It must have realized she wasn't bleeding after all. It sniffed her out, but soon found the true bleeder.

Rachelle reached for her vent valve to plummet, but before she could let out any air, something grabbed her under the arms and swept her up toward the surface.

Jerking her body did nothing to break the hold. A glimpse above only showed another diver. A woman diver. Was she part of a rescue crew? Hope for Gage surged.

Until the woman looked down at her.

Jolene's gray eyes bore down on her with a clear message. *Don't try anything.*

But Gage needed help. He had Marcus *and* a shark to flee from. Rachelle twisted and pulled from Jolene's vise grip. A point downward only got her a head shake. Up and up Jolene took her. As they neared the surface, the water seemed almost foamy. Rachelle remembered the storm coming in.

It appeared it had arrived with torrents of rain, battering the water with pelts of huge drops.

Jolene broke through the surface and dragged Rachelle up behind her. Water stung her cheeks where the mask didn't cover. She let the regulator go from her mouth.

"I have to go back!" Rachelle yelled. "Gage is down there fighting Marcus and a shark, and he's hurt and bleeding!"

No reply came from Jolene. The determined woman swam toward the *Getaway,* dragging Rachelle behind.

"Let me go!"

They reached the ladder at the platform, and Jolene threw her at it. "Climb up!"

"But what about Gage?"

"Girl, there is a shark down there. And I don't mean the animal. I owed you one. That's all you get. Now climb up now!"

Rachelle looked down at the frothy water spraying in drifts around her. If the ladder hadn't been there, she most likely would be pushed under by the huge waves slashing over her.

This was supposed to be a victory, but without Gage it would never be. How could she leave him behind?

In a daze, Rachelle looked around and up to see a hand reaching out to her from the platform. She followed the hand up to its owner. "Owen." The noise around her filtered into her dazed mind.

"Give me your hand, Rachelle!" he yelled down with water dripping from his lips. Had he yelled before and she not heard it?

She gave him her hand and let him lift her out of the

water to land facedown on the platform. After swimming for at least an hour, every single muscle rebelled with tremors. She felt Jolene and Owen removing her buoyancy compensator vest as her face lay on the cold wet platform. Water sloshed around her, mixing with the tears that poured from her eyes. Tears of exhaustion. Tears of guilt. Tears of heartbreak. Tears of defeat.

A whomping sound overhead sounded foreign, and when she opened her eyes, divers were everywhere. A search-and-rescue team, along with a coast guard helicopter hovered above and around her. Help had arrived.

Slowly, Rachelle pushed up on her arms as new hope pushed adrenaline through her muscles. She brought her legs up and flipped over onto her back to watch the rescuers go to work to bring back Gage.

Father God, please lift him out of these deep waters. You've done it before for him. Please, won't You do it again? He is Your faithful servant. He carries Your Word to every shore, bringing hope to the hopeless. He helped wake my mom up from her depressing sleep. But most of all, he made me realize I am loved and treasured by You. Please bring Gage back to me.

"Over here! They're coming up over here!"

Rachelle jumped to her feet and ran to the platform's edge. Her lungs captured her breath as she waited for the rescue divers to emerge.

One came up to the ladder. "We've got one. Almost dead. Tank's empty. He was caught under a cannon."

"Gage? Is it Gage?" Rachelle yelled, but the man shrugged.

Three more divers emerged. *No.* Two more with a man in their arms between them.

It wasn't Gage.

They hoisted Marcus up on the platform. Owen ripped

the mask off him, and none too gently. "Where's Gage?" Owen demanded to his face.

"I...hope..." Marcus caught his breath and began again. "I hope that shark spits him out, so I can kill him again."

One of the divers handed Owen a mask and flipper. "These belonged to the other guy," he said quietly, but Rachelle didn't need him to say anything. She stepped back away and went numb.

A commotion surged around her as Marcus was lifted into the helicopter. She backed up to the railing and turned away from it all. The cold, pelting rain stung her face, but she didn't care.

Gage was dead, and he was never coming back.

"I love you, Gage. I wish I had one more chance to tell you."

"I'm sure he knew." Owen stepped up beside her and rested his hands on the railing, his elbow brushing against hers.

"You're soaked and not wearing a wet suit. You should go inside."

"It's just rain. At least the wind has stopped. I thought the boat would capsize before. I woke up and wished I could knock myself back out again I was so green. You know I'm not one for boats on a good day."

Rachelle knew a bit of Owen's past and how a boating accident left him a widower and a single father. God gave Owen another chance at love and life with Miriam. But first Owen had to learn how to forgive.

"How did you do it?" Rachelle asked in a near whisper. "How did you forgive? It's so hard."

Owen nodded. "Impossible actually. Unless..."

Rachelle searched his face from the corners of her eyes, but knew the answer. "Unless God."

"He'll help you. Trust me. I never would have believed

it myself if Miriam hadn't shown me the light. I'll pray that God will help you, too. Help you forgive your dad and mom, and even Jolene and Marcus."

Rachelle whipped around. "Jolene! Where is she?"

"She's inside. In handcuffs."

"She helped me."

"I know. When I saw her emerge with you, I drew my gun, but then realized she was pulling you to safety. She told me inside that she didn't make the call to Marcus. He'd been trailing her already. When she saw him at your house the day she held your mother and shot at you, she jumped out the window to get away from him. Moved off the boat and hid in the cave right away."

"She's afraid of him."

"Deathly. But she says she'll go quietly to prison and is looking forward to the rest from being under his thumb. She committed a lot of crimes and still needs to pay for them."

Rachelle's shoulders sagged with the weight of Owen's words. The rain slowed to a sprinkle but still doused them as the repercussions of Jolene's and Marcus's choices. "Why? Don't people understand their choices affect everyone around them? Don't they know others will have to pay the consequences? Gage had to die because of their choices." She choked as tears spilled from her eyes at the injustice, but so much more from the loss.

Owen wrapped an arm around her and pulled her head down on his shoulder. Her tears mixed with his soaked shirt until she felt empty. Empty of tears and empty of feeling.

"Watch the rain for a moment, would you?" Owen asked, and she sniffed and lifted her head to stare vacant eyes at the rain pelting the ocean. "Do you see the ripples on the ocean's surface?"

Rachelle sniffed again and nodded.

"Every drop causes a ripple just like our actions. We make a choice, and it affects others. But, Rachelle, it doesn't have to always be a bad thing. A ripple can start with a kind act just as easily as a callous one. In fact, I would say the ripples reach a lot farther when the starting source is a good one."

Rachelle closed her eyes on a sigh and thought of the moment Gage fixed her mom's porch. Violet began to wake up because of it. That ripple changed lives. Rachelle nodded and said, "Gage made a lot of ripples. His goodness reached a lot of people, including me." She opened her eyes to take in the team of people still working to find him. "How long will they continue?"

Owen pressed his lips. "They've already changed the rescue to a recovery. I'm sorry. There's just no way he has air left in his tank."

Rachelle bit her lower lip and wondered how more tears leaked out. "He had no family." She swallowed hard. "He was expected down in Peru for a scout job. Emeralds the size of fists, he said. He could never say no to emeralds. They could lure him in like fish bait across the sea." Rachelle squeezed her eyes as the tears pooled up. "Maybe if I had batted my green eyes at him and asked him not to go to the *Getaway,* he would have listened. He would have stayed with me on the cliffs photographing the hawk. Maybe we would have been caught in the storm and forced to hunker down together on Emerald Point until it passed. Maybe…"

Rachelle felt her heart skip a beat. A flutter of pain or a flicker of hope? She'd chastised Gage for giving people false hope with his Bibles. He had said, there's always hope. For everyone. But how could there be for this situation? He had no air left.

Her heartbeat pounded in her chest and out through her

ears as two words lodged in her throat. Did she dare say
them out loud? What if she was wrong? What if she was
let down again?

It didn't matter. She would still have hope. Always.

"Owen, I think I know where he is."

"Where?"

"Is my boat still here?" Rachelle swept across the platform to find her lobster boat still tied to the *Getaway*.

"Rachelle! Where are you going?"

"Get medical help and meet me at Emerald Point."

"I can't get a boat through there, you know that."

Rachelle cleared the railing of her boat and turned the
engine over. "Yes, you can!" she called back. "There's always hope!"

More than ever before she wished her boat had some
speed. Her fingers drummed on the metal wheel as the engine roared at full speed. A look over her shoulder showed
the large distance she'd already put between her and the
Getaway. Would Gage really have been able to swim this
far?

Keep going, Rachelle. She told herself this, but when
she pushed on with more drive, she had to wonder if God
also championed her.

*Beside me. In front of me. And behind me. Thank You,
God. Lead me to victory.*

The rocks sprang up heavily around her. Anyone of
them could sink her. Many were submerged, and she
wouldn't know her boat scraped along one until it was
too late. Every islander stayed away from this treacherous
place, but Jolene had sailed the *Getaway* in here somehow.
She'd proved it was possible.

The engine rumbled along while Rachelle watched for
dangers and for Gage. The rocks that lay exposed still after
the rain were all empty, but with the darkness looming in,

he could be in the shadows, she thought. She cut the engine and searched the high water with no sight of a person.

Her hopes plummeted. She'd been wrong. He wasn't here, and she would have to accept his death right now. There could be no lighting and extinguishing of this flame. One way or the other, she needed to stand back up on her feet. It's what Gage would want for her. *Your vengeance is your testimony that you got back up.*

And she would get back up for both of them right now. She would stop the ripple of evil meant to destroy them right now. It would not continue with anger or depression. She would send out more ripples, all beginning with good and kind deeds. She would gather up Gage's Bibles and continue his gifts of hope.

And she would pray. She would pray so hard that the good and kind deeds trumped the bad ones. That God would see that their ripples reached farther than any others. And the farther they reached, the more ripples of kindness would branch out from them until everyone felt their touch.

Until everyone felt Gage's touch. His healing touch of hope.

Gage brought goodness and hope, and in his one touch, her life had changed forever. She would carry his ripple on for more to have hope in their lives.

An earsplitting screech wrenched through the air, pulling Rachelle right out of her vindication. She lifted her arms and practically ducked on a gasp as the hawk soared above her.

It swept overhead, and Rachelle watched it in awe, and confusion. "What are you doing out this late? Hunting for prey now?" Rachelle frowned as the hawk became a kindred spirit. "No. You're looking for your mate, aren't you? I know the feeling, and I'm so sorry."

The hawk flew back toward shore with a swoop down

and up in perfect aerodynamics. Her beauty and agility awed Rachelle. She felt a little trepidation when the bird flew back in her direction. She aimed down like a flying torpedo, and Rachelle dived down to the deck of the wheelhouse. The bird dashed back up to the sky and soared toward her nest.

Unsure of what the aerial show had been about, Rachelle followed the path the bird had taken, from where she swept down near the shore over the empty rocks.

Except one of the rocks on the shore just moved.

Rocks don't move, she told herself and anchored her boat to dive overboard. Stroke after stroke she pushed through until her feet found ground. The water slowed her as she tried to run with giant strides. Soon she reached the rock. And compared to the rock wall she'd climbed earlier, these things were skipping stones.

Rachelle climbed up with her feet following her hands until her hands hit a leg.

"Gage!" She pulled her body the rest of the way up to lay beside him. "Gage, are you hurt?" She dared not touch him and cause more damage, but he did manage to pull himself up on this rock, so that was a good sign.

"You're alive," Gage moaned with his cheek against the rock. "Thank God, you're alive. I thought—"

"Shh," Rachelle cupped his cheek and leaned down to kiss his cheek, then forehead, then his cheek again. She felt his smile as his laugh lines popped out under her lips.

"What's this all about?" He struggled to turn on his side under the weight of his gear, and possibly an injury.

She lifted her head. "They're kisses of joy that you're alive. Now don't move. Help is on the way."

"I won't turn the docs away, but I think I'm okay. Just wiped out. The tank's bone dry. I can't believe I made it."

"Why, Gage, I'm surprised in you. Aren't you the one full of faith and hope?"

"Yes, but neither of those matter without love. I now understand why it's the greatest of them. When I thought I'd lost you, I felt like my hope vented out of me like the last of my air."

"No, Gage. It didn't. God wouldn't have left you. You may have been knocked down, but you would have stood back up and gone on. You would have sailed on to your next shipwreck and touched more lives with the hope you bring to their shores. In the same way you touched mine."

Gage reached out a slow, weak hand and cupped her cheek. His thumb rubbed gently across her cheekbones. His warm breath hit her chin as he exhaled. "You're amazing, *mi joya*. So brave and strong."

"No, I've been rescued, and now I'm free. There is power in freedom, and God is going to use you to bring more people to victory."

Gage frowned and dropped his hand from her face. "Why do I get the feeling you're sending me away? First of all, my engines are cooked. I'm not going anywhere for a while. Sorry if that upsets you."

"Why would that upset me?"

"Well, you sure got upset when I told you I loved you. Now you're already planning my bon voyage party."

"I wasn't angry at you. Well, at first I was because I didn't think you meant it."

"Of course, you didn't, my little skeptic."

"Just listen," Rachelle demanded. "I was mad because you told me you loved me, and I would never hear your most precious words with my own ears. Marcus was about to kill us, and I would never hear how your words settled around my heart and brought me peace. How they imprinted into my brain as a forever memory I could pull on for the rest of my life. I vowed in the water right then that I would do everything I could to make sure we both made it out alive. I vowed I would hear your voice as you professed those words to me, and I would hold them in my heart forever." Rachelle dropped her forehead to his, peering through her eyelashes, her emerald eyes locked on his sky-blues. "I was also mad because I would never get the chance to tell you that…I loved you."

Gage's eyes drifted closed on another exhale. "I see what you mean. My heart just skipped at the sound of those words. I don't think I've ever felt anything so right." He opened his eyes and pushed himself up to a sitting position. His good hand reached for hers, intertwining their fingers. He squeezed tight and released as though he'd come to a decision. "I'll do my best to be a good fisherman. I'll make you proud, and I'd be honored to call Stepping Stones my home."

Rachelle leaned back and tilted her head. "Those weren't really the words I was looking for, and I'm not looking to hire you. Did you hear me? I said, I love you."

"But Rachelle, how can I ask you to marry me if I don't even have a job?"

"How can you ask me to marry you if you won't even tell me you love me? And you do have a job. Aren't you needed down in Peru to scout for another wreck? Something about emeralds and their ability to draw you across oceans."

"Emeralds! I almost forgot." He unzipped a pouch on his BC vest and reached in. "I figured out why they call this place Emerald Point." He withdrew his hand and opened it palm up.

"Is that a real emerald?" She picked up the golf ball sized stone covered in muck. It didn't look very pretty at the moment.

"It sure is. There might even be some more down there the pirates lost or forgot. Your islanders should be pretty happy. I found it as I ascended right below on one of the rocks, sitting there all pretty on a ledge. A great hiding place some pirate found."

She twisted her lips. "You think this is pretty?"

"Give her a break. She was just rescued. We don't all rise up from rock bottom looking adorable like yourself."

Rachelle smiled at his twinkling eyes. "You're getting warmer, but you still haven't said you love me. Oh, I know! Maybe we could use this to buy new engines for the *Getaway*. I'm sure the islanders would all agree, and that way we could leave right away and you wouldn't be late for your job."

"No, Rachelle, I could never take you off your land."

"But the *Getaway*'s your home. As soon as your engines are repaired you can set out with the sea breeze blowing in your face as you sail right into the sun."

Gage chuckled. "Is that how you imagine me at the helm? Sounds dreamy, but not practical. Manning a yacht alone isn't so glorious. It's a lot of work. Hard work that requires movement from stem to stern, day in and day out."

"Then you should get yourself a first mate. Consider this my application."

"Are you serious? You would really sail around the world with me?"

"Only if you loved me. And, I'm still waiting."

"But what about your mom and your photography?"

"We would visit Stepping Stones and I'm in the market for an underwater camera. There's a whole world down there to be captured. Even that shark was stunning. If I can angle the lens just right, I could get a shot looking right into its round, black eye, so the creature could tell me its story."

Gage's mouth dropped in stunned silence. "Are you

saying you'll dive again? After everything that's happened to you?"

"With you as my teacher, of course. What kind of fish do you think I'll see in Peru?"

"I love you," he said.

Rachelle grinned from ear to ear. "And there it is! I feel it right here." She placed her hand over her heart. "All warm and fuzzy."

"I love you," Gage repeated as he reached up behind her neck and pulled her forehead to his. "I love you. I love you. I love you."

Her smile descended from her lips as his words sank in. Each time he repeated the words, they touched a different part of her as his love rippled through her. First, her heart where a warming sensation made her smile. Then, her mind where his words erased any skepticism that lingered there about her decision to set sail with him. Her soul where joy filled her at finding her lifelong mate came next. And finally, her feet where sure footing was found. Together they would stand rescued, freed and victorious.

"Hey, you two," A voice spoke through a bullhorn from sea, and they turned to see Owen on his sheriff's boat. "It looks like everything's all right here. Do you need anything, Gage?"

"Just this woman's hand in marriage!" Gage shouted back.

Owen laughed and spoke through his bullhorn, "Rachelle's a good judge of character and knows when to keep them and when to throw them back in, but if you don't mind, I'm going to bail on this one. Glad to have you back, Captain." Owen mock saluted him and hit Reverse.

Gage squeezed her hand, pulling her attention back to him. "Rachelle, you've already honored me with your willingness to share my life and everything I love, but without you as my bride, none of it matters. Would you give me one more honor? The biggest honor of them all. Would you marry me?"

"Do I get to be first mate as we hunt for treasure?" She batted her eyelashes with a smile.

"First, second, third or whatever you want. I'll even make you captain. You know I've never been able to say no to emeralds." He leaned in to kiss her but halted a breath away from her lips. He waited for her answer, she knew, and she wasn't sure she could bait him much longer.

She studied his expectant lips and wanted him to kiss her more than anything else. She leaned forward, but he inched away. "It would seem I've been caught in my own trap."

"Then say yes, so I can claim the only treasure I care about."

Rachelle sighed with a nod and a sting of tears in her eyes. "Yes, Gage. I will marry you. I will stand beside you at the helm through every purple and tangerine sunrise and through every rocky storm that comes our way. Always and forever. Now kiss me."

"Aye-aye, Captain," he said as he caught her up in his arms and fulfilled his orders.

* * * * *

Dear Reader,

Thank you for joining me on Stepping Stones Island, where the lobster traps are always full and romance awaits even the hardest of hearts. Especially, with Gage Fontaine sailing into port. His buoyant joy for life had Rachelle's skepticism flying at full mast. Her baggage of shame and bitterness loaded onto her by her father and his crimes has left her suspicious of people's motives, even her own.

But Gage sees the treasure she really is and knows God is searching for her like a lost coin. A coin more valuable than the coins Gage has traveled to Stepping Stones to find far below the ocean's surface. Stepping Stones Island's history included pirates, and now because of him, unfortunately, it does again.

It's a map of excitement and danger Gage and Rachelle had to navigate, and I do hope you buckled up for the bumpy parts of the ride.

Thank you for reading! I love hearing from readers. You can visit my website, www.KatyLeeBooks.com, or email me at KatyLee@KatyLeeBooks.com. If you don't have internet access, you can write to me c/o Love Inspired Books, 233 Broadway, Suite 1001, New York, NY 10279.

Katy Lee

Questions for Discussion

1. How did Rachelle deal with her father's arrest? What did she fear that would make her react in this way?

2. Rachelle saw Gage's optimism as naive and believed him to be either a fraud or too privileged to understand what rock bottom felt like. Why couldn't she believe in his sense of hope?

3. How did you feel about Gage when he first came on the scene? Did you trust him when it appeared he was affiliated with modern-day piracy?

4. Movies and literature can portray piracy as romantic, but it really was—and is—quite violent. What do you know about modern-day piracy and our military's response?

5. Rachelle wanted vengeance against Jolene for shooting at her, but Gage knew there was another way to achieve restitution. What was it?

6. What did Gage see in Rachelle when he began to get to know her?

7. What were some of the ways Gage helped Rachelle see she was needed and important in her community?

8. Depression hurts whole families. The person suffering with depression is not the only one to feel its effects. How did Rachelle feel watching her mother battle with this condition?

9. Rachelle accuses Gage of giving people false hope when he travels to countries bringing Bibles. He tells her there is hope for all, but she only sees the evil in the world and the ways innocent people pay for it. What is one thing Gage does for her to show her there really is hope?

10. Our actions come with ripple effects. We can focus on the ripples started by bad things, or we can focus on the ones started by good. What are some good ripples you can start that will reach out to the world and bring hope?

11. What was your favorite scene in the story, and why?

12. Gage's theme in the story is Psalm 18:16. "He reached down from heaven and rescued me. He lifted me out of deep waters." What does this scripture mean for you?

13. Gage gave his life to Jesus at seventeen when he turned his back on the evil life he was heading into. He knew God rescued him, and he gave his life to his Savior, but Gage still had the consequences of his past choices chasing him. He allowed it to continue, because he felt as though he deserved these chains. Do you have something from your past still chasing you? God wants to free you. Will you let Him?

14. Rachelle's community and friends loved her, but in her pain and shame she retreated from them. In doing so, she allowed a year to go by essentially hiding from them. Who did her choices hurt? Are you in hiding for something not dealt with in your life? How can you end that today?

15. Diving is something Rachelle feared until she was forced to do it. Now she looks forward to her many dives to come with Gage. Is there anything in your life you're afraid to try? What is stopping you?

REQUEST YOUR FREE BOOKS!
2 FREE RIVETING INSPIRATIONAL NOVELS
PLUS 2 FREE MYSTERY GIFTS

Love Inspired®
SUSPENSE

YES! Please send me 2 FREE Love Inspired® Suspense novels and my 2 FREE mystery gifts (gifts are worth about $10). After receiving them, if I don't wish to receive any more books, I can return the shipping statement marked "cancel." If I don't cancel, I will receive 4 brand-new novels every month and be billed just $4.74 per book in the U.S. or $5.24 per book in Canada. That's a savings of at least 21% off the cover price. It's quite a bargain! Shipping and handling is just 50¢ per book in the U.S. and 75¢ per book in Canada.* I understand that accepting the 2 free books and gifts places me under no obligation to buy anything. I can always return a shipment and cancel at any time. Even if I never buy another book, the two free books and gifts are mine to keep forever.

123/323 IDN F5AC

Name	(PLEASE PRINT)
Address	Apt. #
City	State/Prov.	Zip/Postal Code

Signature (if under 18, a parent or guardian must sign)

Mail to the Harlequin® Reader Service:
IN U.S.A.: P.O. Box 1867, Buffalo, NY 14240-1867
IN CANADA: P.O. Box 609, Fort Erie, Ontario L2A 5X3

Are you a current subscriber to Love Inspired Suspense books and want to receive the larger-print edition?
Call 1-800-873-8635 or visit www.ReaderService.com.

* Terms and prices subject to change without notice. Prices do not include applicable taxes. Sales tax applicable in N.Y. Canadian residents will be charged applicable taxes. Offer not valid in Quebec. This offer is limited to one order per household. Not valid for current subscribers to Love Inspired Suspense books. All orders subject to credit approval. Credit or debit balances in a customer's account(s) may be offset by any other outstanding balance owed by or to the customer. Please allow 4 to 6 weeks for delivery. Offer available while quantities last.

Your Privacy—The Harlequin® Reader Service is committed to protecting your privacy. Our Privacy Policy is available online at www.ReaderService.com or upon request from the Harlequin Reader Service.
We make a portion of our mailing list available to reputable third parties that offer products we believe may interest you. If you prefer that we not exchange your name with third parties, or if you wish to clarify or modify your communication preferences, please visit us at www.ReaderService.com/consumerschoice or write to us at Harlequin Reader Service Preference Service, P.O. Box 9062, Buffalo, NY 14269. Include your complete name and address.

LIS13R

SPECIAL EXCERPT FROM

Love Inspired
SUSPENSE

Danger and love go hand in hand in the small town
of Wrangler's Corner. Read on for a sneak preview of
THE LAWMAN RETURNS by Lynette Eason,
the first book in this exciting new series from
Love Inspired Suspense.

Sheriff's deputy Clay Starke wheeled to a stop in front of
the beat-up trailer. He heard the sharp crack, and the side
of the trailer spit metal.

A shooter.

The woman on the porch careened down the steps and
bolted toward him. Terror radiated from her. He shoved
open the door to the passenger side. "Get in!"

Breathless, she landed in the passenger seat and slammed
the door. Eyes wide, she lifted shaking hands to push her
blond hair out of her eyes.

Clay got on his radio and reported shots fired.

He cranked the car and started to back out of the drive.

"No! We can't leave!"

"What?" He stepped on the brake. "Lady, if someone's
shooting, I'm getting you out of here."

"But I think Jordan's in there, and I can't leave without
him."

"Jordan?"

"A boy I work with. He called me for help. I'm worried
he might be hurt."

Clay put the car back in Park. "Then stay down and let
me check it out."

"But if you get out, he might shoot you."

He waited. No more shots. "Stay put. I think he might be gone."

"Or waiting for one of us to get out of the car."

True. He could feel her gaze on him, studying him, dissecting him. He frowned. "What is it?"

"You."

He shot a glance behind them, then let his gaze rove the area until he'd gone in a full circle and was once again looking into her pretty face. "What about me?"

Red crept into her cheeks. "You look so much like Steven. Are you related?"

He stilled, focusing in on her. "I'm Clay Starke. You knew my brother?"

"Clay? I'm Sabrina Mayfield."

Oh, wow. Sabrina Mayfield. "Are you saying the kid in there knows something about Steven's death?"

"I don't know what he's doing here, but he called me and said he thought he knew who killed Steven and he needed me to come get him."

A tingle of shock raced through Clay. Finally. After weeks with nothing, this could be the break he'd been looking for. "Then I want to know what he knows."

Pick up THE LAWMAN RETURNS, available October 2014 wherever Love Inspired Suspense books are sold.

Love Inspired

SUSPENSE

RIVETING INSPIRATIONAL ROMANCE

AROUND-THE-CLOCK PROTECTOR

Despite the threats against her life, Danielle Barclay thinks having a bodyguard is unnecessary. Or at least that's what she tells herself before meeting Jake Rabb. A former Delta Force solider, Jake is used to rope-lining from helicopters into enemy territory–not following around a senator's daughter. The lovely deputy district attorney is as strong-willed as she is brave, especially when the escalating danger assures Jake that her stalker means business. As the attacks become personal, Danielle finally puts her trust–and her feelings–on the line with her defender. But how will Jake protect her if the stalker is closer than they think?

KEEPING WATCH
by
JANE M. CHOATE

Available October 2014 wherever
Love Inspired books and ebooks are sold.

LIS44629